Under the Cottonwoods
and other Mormon stories

Under the Cottonwoods
and other Mormon stories

DOUGLAS H. THAYER

FRANKSON
·BOOKS·

Library of Congress Cataloging in Publication Data

Thayer, Douglas H   1929-
    Under the cottonwoods and other Mormon stories.

    1. Mormons and Mormonism — Fiction. I. Title.
PZ4.T372Un [PS3570.H346]   813'.5'4   77-1210

Library of Congress Catalog Card Number: 77-1210

Printed in the United States of America by Press
Publishing Limited

Book design and illustration by Ron Eddington

Published by Frankson Books
Box 7090, University Station
Provo, Utah 84602

For Donlu

The previously published stories in this collection appear by permission:

"The Rabbit Hunt," *Brigham Young University Studies* (Winter, 1969).

"Opening Day," *Dialogue: A Journal of Mormon Thought* (Spring, 1970).

"Second South," *Dialogue: A Journal of Mormon Thought* (Winter, 1970).

"Testimony." An earlier version of this story appeared in *The Ensign* (May, 1971) under the title "The First Sunday."

"Under the Cottonwoods," *Dialogue: A Journal of Mormon Thought* (Autumn, 1972).

"Zarahemla." An earlier version of this story appeared in *Brigham Young University Studies* (Winter, 1974).

"Greg." *Dialogue: A Journal of Mormon Thought* (Autumn, 1976).

CONTENTS

SECOND SOUTH

Sitting back Philip felt the vibration of the train through his feet, and if he leaned forward a little he saw tops of heads and the silver sign that said "MEN" in black letters. The little blond boy who had gotten on at Denver came lurching down the aisle to sit by him again, but his mother said, "Don't bother the soldier any more right now, honey." He wouldn't tell Philip his name. The sagebrush flats and gullies were full of the early evening shadows. After the train stopped at Price it would climb to the summit, drop down Spanish Fork Canyon into the valley to Springville, then Provo, and he would be home. The conductor came down the aisle, his gold watch chain in two loops across his fat stomach. Philip turned to look out the window again. In three hours he would be home and tomorrow was Sunday. Hanging from the baggage rack, his clean summer uniform swung gently.

When he thought about being home he felt something almost like pain. After his return from Germany and his discharge at Camp Kilmer three days before, he had gone straight to New York City to get a train.

1

And he had walked down the New York streets only as far as he could keep Grand Central Station in sight. He was afraid that he might get lost and miss his train, get hit by a taxi, or be arrested. For two years he had dreamed about coming home to Utah, a thousand times pictured the Wasatch Mountains, the valley, Provo, Second South, the trees, green lawns with the sprays going, the clean water in the ditches, their white house. He heard his father calling in his two younger brothers, Allen and Mark, listened to his mother fixing the before-bed piece of cake or dish of bottled fruit in the kitchen. And he saw the Sixth Ward chapel, heard the singing on Sunday morning, everybody calling each other brother and sister, the girls lovely and clean in their Sunday dresses. He longed to return to all those things that were familiar, good, beautiful, and clean, leave Germany. Holding his two hands in his, palms up, his father had said to him on his last furlough, "Keep safe, son, and come home clean."

A white-jacketed waiter came through announcing the second call for supper. Philip stood up. He had waited purposely; supper would take nearly an hour if he ate slowly. Stopping in the men's room, he washed his face and hands and combed his hair. Later he would put on his clean uniform. He had made corporal and the family wanted to see him in his uniform before he took it off for good. His mother wrote that he should wait until he got home to buy his new civilian clothes so that she could go with him uptown to Taylor Brothers. The family didn't know just when he would arrive, and he was going to surprise them.

With a flick of his long yellow pencil the steward pointed him to an empty chair across the table from a sailor with two rows of combat ribbons. Rick, the sailor, told him what great occupation duty Japan was, how he hated to leave the geishas, soft job, easy black-market money, saki, the baths and massages, everything. He wanted to know if Germany was really as terrific as they said. Did the Germans still have plenty of jewelry, cameras, and binoculars left, and would they sell anything for food, or was the German black market already shot? Could you keep one of those beautiful German blonde frauleins for just one pack of cigarettes a day? Were the German broads really just like stateside women? Gripping the cold filmy water glass, Philip stared out the window into the growing darkness. He got Rick talking about his ribbons.

When they stopped at Price, the little boy and his mother walked up and down on the platform through the squares of light from the diner windows. He looked up at Philip and waved. His mother took him by the hand to get back on the train, but he kept waving. Leaning back in his chair to light a cigarette, Rick wanted to know if he and the boy were related. The train pulled out of Price and started climbing toward the summit.

After Philip got back to his car he washed his hands, brushed his teeth, combed his hair, and then went up in the vista-dome. A few stars were out. The dome rocked like a boat at sea, and people were quieter than down below. Rich had started it all again for him, everything that he had tried to forget, the pictures he wanted to hold from his mind. Germany. Lying back in his seat he stared out through the curved vista-dome glass.

He had landed in Bremerhaven aboard the U.S.S.

3

Ballou, a liberty ship, on an evening in early January. It was snowing. Because the train they boarded the next morning was poorly heated, they wore their overcoats, gloves, and hats. All through high school he had heard the radio reports, seen the war movies and newsreels, but now he could hardly believe that he was in Germany. He stared out the window all day at the destroyed bridges, exploded locomotives, and broken boxcars along the tracks, the burned-out German half-tracks and tanks lying near the roads. Bordered by walls of black pines, the white fields were empty of cattle, the villages lifeless, the cities vast piles of snow-covered rubble. Except for the children who spread their gloveless red hands against the windows and begged for food, few people were in the stations. When it grew dark no lights burned inside or outside of the train, and it was like riding in a long tunnel.

They arrived in Frankfurt the next evening and were trucked through the dark snow-covered streets to Able Area, a fenced compound of yellow former German army barracks, where they still wore their coats because it was so cold. After he had unpacked his duffel bag into the high wooden German wall locker, Philip stood and looked out the third-story window. Scattered in twos and threes, black against the snow, many women walked outside the high barbed-wire fence under the guard lights. Their breath white, they stood in small bunches to talk to the GIs who stood at open windows.

Beyond the fence it was dark. Reynolds, a short bald corporal who bunked in the same five-man room, put his hand on his shoulder. "Take your pick, kid," he said; "all you need is this." And he held up a package of Camel cigarettes and motioned toward the women. A GI walked up to one of the women, spoke to her, and they walked away together. "See." Reynolds turned his face from the window. "How old are you, kid?" He said that he had just turned eighteen. He had joined the army for the GI Bill so that he could go to college and become a teacher. "Oh good hell, just eighteen." Reynolds gripped his shoulder tighter and asked him where he was from.

That night when he was in bed under four blankets and his overcoat and still cold, he heard Reynolds say, "You're in the promised land, kid. Lots of frauleins. I'll help you." The women begged for chocolate, soap, cigarettes, anything that they could eat or could barter on the black market for food or fuel. The Germans were starving and freezing. The women invited the GIs to come out, beckoned, made a play at climbing the fence, and then fought for what was thrown. But Reynolds said that a big redhead always won if she was around. There were sixty or seventy women, and some of them were old.

Able Area housed a service battalion, and he was assigned as a clerk-typist in the Provost Marshall's Section, European Command, where the thirty other GIs worked that bunked at his end of the hall. All but two of them had German girl friends. Every night after work the men ate supper, filled their canvas bags with PX items and food they stole from the mess hall, and left, going down the hall laughing, describing what they had in the bag tonight. Reynolds told him that he was nuts not to have a fraulein, urged him, and said that he could arrange it, but Philip shook his head. When the section found out he was from Utah, they wanted to know how many wives his father had.

Each night he polished his brass, his shoes,

5

pressed his pants for the next day, often swept and mopped the room. And he hunched near the radiator in his overcoat to study German for his USAFI course, read library books, and to look up Book of Mormon scriptures that his mother noted in her letters. He watched the women walking outside the fence, but he never opened his window. No matter how cold the water was he always showered, then, feeling clean, prayed lying in bed. Later, staring up at the white ceiling, he listened to the GIs returning, some drunk, their loud voices muffled behind the latrine door. Reynolds said nearly every night, "Kid, you just don't know what you're missing. It ain't natural." He didn't go to the monthly section parties and he wouldn't buy his cigarette ration to sell on the black market. They thought that he was crazy, called him Virginia, shouted it in front of his door at night, laughed, opened the door just enough to poke their heads in and say softly, "V-i-r-g-i-n-i-a."

He played ping-pong at the Red Cross Club with a GI named Simmons or they went to the movie, but mostly he was alone. Often he stared out the window at the grey spring clouds, the rain, the horizon without mountains, and at the ruins. The ruins made him feel more than any other thing that he had left the world he knew. From the trolley he saw the blocks of rubble, with only halves and quarters of buildings standing. There were walls where pictures still hung and curtains fluttered at windows. Old people, some crying, cupping their white faces with their hands, stood before the crosses planted in the red mounds of brick. He copied the notes tacked to the doors of blasted houses, **and** later, using his German dictionary, read of chil-**dre**n burned alive, whole families killed, buried still.

Sometimes he saw people digging into the mounds, but he didn't walk far into the ruins. Gangs of boys lived in the cellars hidden under the rubble, and when they couldn't steal they hunted the cats for food.

The desire to return home was like a vague sickness. At night he lay and imagined himself back in Provo, saw pictures on the white ceiling—the green valley, the high Wasatch Mountains surrounding everything. He cut the lawn, roughhoused with Mark and Allen, ate supper, helped his mother with the dishes, talked to his father on the front porch, walked a girl up to Hedquist's Drug Store for a malt. He went to church at the Sixth Ward, shook hands, called everybody brother and sister, sang "Come, Come, Ye Saints," "We Thank Thee, O God, For A Prophet," "Zion Stands With Hills Surrounded." Or he saw himself discharged, going home, walking down Second South under the trees, the joy so strong in him that he wanted to drop his duffel bag and run shouting down the street. Over and over he planned how it would be.

Lying in his bunk in the morning, awake in the silent barracks, he stared up at the white ceiling again before he got up. He was always first down to the latrine. If all the sinks contained cigarette butts, vomit or used prophylactic kits, the little green tubes squeezed flat, he showered again, brushed his teeth under the clean spray. Twice a week he shaved.

Saturdays he watched the baseball games (Reynolds managed their team), went swimming often, and in August took a Special Services tour to Luxembourg for three days. Mrs. Thatcher, who lived two houses down from his family, wanted him to visit her son's grave in a military cemetery there, and his mother wrote that it would be a nice thing for him to do. Bob had played football in high school, owned an old yellow Model-A Ford, and was a lifeguard at the North Park swimming pool during the summer. After he took the pictures, Philip looked down at the wreath on the green grass by the cross and wondered if he should salute. The cemetery wasn't finished, but already there were acres and acres of white markers.

When he got back to Frankfurt he thought about the German soldiers who had lived in his room, and he searched all the walls and the furniture looking for a name. Because there was no servicemen's branch of the Church where he was, he went to Protestant services and in the choir sang the unfamiliar hymns. The chaplain found out for him where the nearest German military cemetery was located, and he went there one Sunday afternoon, walked from marker to marker reading the names aloud. And after that Sunday he began throwing soap and candy to the women at the fence. When the big redhead got the soap she pantomimed taking a bath, gestured for him to come with her, but he shook his head and she laughed. He made battalion soldier of the week two weeks straight and his mother had it put in the Provo *Daily Herald*. She said that he was being a fine example for other boys. His bishop wrote to congratulate him and asked how soon he wanted to go on a mission when he returned home.

Something touched Philip's knee, and he turned from the vista-dome window. The little blond boy looked up at him. "Can I sit up there too, soldier?" he asked. Later his mother came to the stairs and called him back. Across the canyon, headlights moved along the highway.

8

That fall he drove the weapons carrier for the monthly section parties. There had been an accident and they needed a driver who didn't drink. They wouldn't leave him alone about it; they said that it would do him good. Some of the frauleins were pretty, but most had flat, plain faces, and after they danced a faint sour odor rose from their unwashed bodies. Even with the GIs leaning over to kiss them, they ate and drank, the room full of grey cigarette smoke. When the GIs said that they called him Virginia and explained what it meant, the frauleins screamed, and when he refused to dance they raised their glasses to him. After he drove the couples home, clinging together, they lurched down the alleys or fumbled for keys at the high wooden doors facing the streets. The frauleins turned to yell for him to come too because they had a roommate, and he understood the German words mixed in with the English. The patched and broken windows glimmered in the weapons carrier headlights, and the moon shone down on the ruined buildings.

At Christmas his friends and relatives in Provo sent cards and said how they looked forward to his safe return in August. His mother wrote that nothing had changed in the neighborhood except that some new apartments would be built on Third West that summer. Christmas Eve he stood in the warm barracks room watching the women below digging in the deep snow for the candy bars and soap he had thrown out to them. He knew several of them by sight now, and somehow they had learned his name. They yelled, "Philip! Philip!" in a different German way until he came to the window and threw them something. One woman brought her two little girls.

He knew that the Germans still went hungry. He remembered the children pressing their red palms against the train windows begging for food and the boys he saw in the ruins cooking something in an old GI helmet. Every evening the nuns still came to get the mess-hall scraps for the orphanage. One night the green GI can tipped from their sled and he helped them gather the bones, pieces of dry bread, and chunks of boiled potatoes from the snow. He said *bitte schön* when they thanked him, then stood there to watch the wind whip their black clothes as they went out through the gate. Behind them walked four GIs carrying their canvas bags. That night, staring up at the white ceiling, he prayed for the children and the nuns.

When he received his orders to return to the States for discharge, the section celebrated at the July party. Crowding around him, laughing, shouting, they forced him to drink one toast, and the schnaps was like fire in him. Each of the frauleins clamored to dance with him, embracing him, whirling him across the floor through the grey smoke-filled air, laughing. He felt the warm damp flesh of their hands, their soft breasts against his chest, their thighs against his. He had to sit down between dances once, squeeze his arms tight around his stomach and bend over against the feeling. The frauleins shrieked with laughter. "See what you been missing, kid?" Reynolds stood before him, his white bald head glistening with sweat. "You've missed a lot, kid . . . everything. You should re-enlist." The next day he bought $20 worth of soap and candy at the PX and gave it all to the women at the fence that night.

The big red-headed woman laughed and said,

"You go home? You go home?"

Philip stared out through the vista-dome glass at the squares of light from the windows racing along the ground with the train. They passed Soldier Summit, where his father always stopped on their way back from fishing at Scofield Reservoir to buy him and his brothers a root beer. And then later, far below down Spanish Fork Canyon, he saw the glimmering patches of light on the valley floor. Provo was the largest town in the valley and the only passenger train stop. The top of his mouth ached and his eyes stung. That afternoon when they crossed from Colorado into Utah and he saw the marker on the cliff, he had felt the same way.

He walked back to his car past the quiet passengers, got his suitcase, his clean summer uniform, and went to the men's room. The little blond boy followed him until his mother said, "Come back, honey. Don't bother the soldier." The rest room was empty. He pulled the curtain tight against the edges of the door, washed, shaved, brushed his teeth, combed his hair, and then put on his clean uniform and changed his socks. He wanted to take a good hot shower and put on clean shorts. He swallowed hard when he thought what a terrific surprise it would be for everybody when he walked up the front steps. Just as he started to polish his shoes, the conductor came in and sat down on the black leather couch. Grey cigar ashes caught in the wrinkles of his vest below the gold chain.

"Just get discharged, corporal?"

"Yes."

"Get overseas?"

"Germany."

"I could tell by the shoulder patch. That must have been real nice for a young buck like you."

11

Philip put the shoeshine kit back in his suitcase.

"I was there after the first war." He puffed on his cigar, filling the room with blue smoke. "It was a great life then too, easy money on the black market, all the schnaps a man could want, and lots of frauleins." The conductor leaned back into the couch. "You can't beat those German frauleins can you, corporal, you just can't beat 'em." The conductor kept looking up at him, smiling.

"I guess not." He put his dirty uniform and socks in his suitcase and then washed his hands again.

"I guess not." The conductor laughed. "You know I still got the camera and binoculars I picked up over there. The Germans make the best optics in the world." The conductor stood up and followed him to the curtain. "Wish we could have shot the bull a little. Brings back a lot of memories." The conductor started to laugh again. "Oh, if the little wife only knew."

Philip went back to his seat, but he didn't sit down because he didn't want to wrinkle his uniform. They went through Springville. "Provo, Provo next stop." The conductor gripped his arm as he passed. Reaching up to get his duffel bag from the rack, Philip felt himself sway forward as the train slowed. His heart pounded in his throat and his hands sweat. They passed the Provo cemetery, the white crosses and tombstones gleaming in the moonlight.

The air was cool and dry when he stepped into the station, the sky clear and full of stars and the moon. He turned to look up at the train as it pulled out. The little blond boy waved to him, the palm of his left hand pressed white against the window. The conductor leaned out over the half-door and said something, but there was too much noise. It was something about

12

American girls. Philip set his duffel bag down and waved to the little blond boy until the long aluminum car curved around the bend and he vanished.

Philip stood there watching the red lights on the end of the last car until they disappeared into the darkness, then he picked up his bag and went inside the station. The agent, who knew his father, shook his hand through the window. "Glad to see you back, son," he said. "Pick up your bag any time, no charge. Always glad to have you boys get home again safe and sound."

"Thank you, sir," he said.

Philip trembled when he got outside. He saw the Wasatch Mountains against the sky, the canopy of trees over the sidewalk up Third West, the neat houses and lawns, the silver water in the ditch. The suitcase slapping his leg, he could run the three blocks to Second South, turn the corner, go charging up the front steps, shout, "Mom! Dad! I'm home! I'm home!" but he wouldn't. Already his body tingled, and he wanted to feel every step. He passed Webster's Corner Grocery store, the big yellow Camel cigarette sign painted on the side, and he stopped before the dark window to comb his hair. A robin flew away as he passed and the mist from the lawn sprays cooled him. The lawns were all cut for Sunday, and all up the street the lawn sprays were silver in the light from the porches and street lamps. After he crossed Fourth South he knew some of the people sitting on the porches and he nodded when they said hello, but he didn't stop. Standing in a doorway, a girl in a white dress watched him walk by. He would know everybody after he turned on his street. Some of the older children played tag, a baby cried then hushed, and

13

from somewhere came the sound of soft radio music. When he crossed Third South he saw the front of the Sixth Ward chapel and above the trees the dark blue silhouette of the mountains again.

Walking under the trees, he passed the sign advertising the new apartments his mother had written about. Roofs gone, and some walls, the bricks and plaster in piles of rubble, three houses were being torn down. The bathtubs, washbasins, sinks and toilets lay white under the single light burning near the piles of salvage. Then from the ruined houses he heard a girl laugh softly, laugh again, louder, and he stopped. A boy and girl, arms around each other, came out of the side door of the middle house. The girl stopped to pull her dress straight and brush it off with her hand. The boy lit a cigarette and then held it away from the girl when she reached for it. "Oh, come on, honey," she said, "you ought to be nice to me." He laughed, handed her the cigarette, pushed back her long red hair and kissed her on the neck. After he lit another cigarette, he put his arm around her shoulder and they crossed the street, her long hair shimmering.

Philip turned and walked slowly up to the corner, paused, turned, walked up Second South a few steps and put down his suitcase. Three houses further on the lawn spray was going under the big willow tree in front of their house. Across the street, Mr. and Mrs. Johnson sat on their front porch watching two boys playing catch in the street. The boys were Mark and Allen, his brothers. He saw his father come down their front steps and move the lawn sprinkler, then stand to say something to the Johnsons. His mother walked down the steps to his father and he put his arm around her shoulders. Reaching down, Philip picked up his

14

suitcase, but stood for a moment. And then, under the dark green trees, the shadows filtering over him as he passed, he walked slowly toward them. His father still had his arm around his mother's shoulders.

OPENING DAY

Doc and my father got up at 4 o'clock to light the fire, heat water on the Coleman stoves for washing and get the breakfast started, then woke the rest of us. Standing outside of our white tent in the cool darkness, I buckled on my heavy cartridge belt and breathed in deep the smell of wood smoke and sagebrush. I looked down Blind Canyon and then turned to look up at the black silhouette of the ridge under the stars. I knew the bucks would already be out feeding in the draws. The ridge ran east and west, and we hunted the draws on the south and north slopes. I still felt the old excitement of the opening day of the deer hunt, an empty tight feeling as if my whole body were being squeezed. I still wanted to see the big mule-deer bucks jump out of the oak brush ahead of the line, shoot them as they ran. But then I hadn't expected to have absolute control over my emotions just because while I was on my mission in Germany I had decided to stop hunting. When I got married and had sons, I didn't want them to hunt, but I knew that it wouldn't be easy for me to stop killing birds and animals.

17

Bliss, Dean, and Ken stood by the fire, and Jerry washed in the pan of warm water on the end of the table. The light from the fire and the two Coleman lanterns glared off from their red hats, sweat shirts, and jackets. When they moved, the handles of their hunting knives, aluminum lids of their old GI belt canteens, and the shells in their full cartridge belts glinted.

When the rest of us had washed, Doc asked me to give the morning prayer and blessing on the food, said that we had to keep the returned missionaries busy. After we ate we got our rifles out of the cases in the tent, saddled Bliss's three horses, and put the lunches and the two walkie-talkies in the saddlebags. We turned off the lanterns, shoveled dirt on the fire, and we were ready, each of us carrying his rifle slung. My father, Doc, and Bliss, who were older and worked on the Union Pacific Railroad together, rode the horses, the rest of us following in single file across the sagebrush flat to the start of the trail at the base of the ridge. Every hundred yards we had to stop to rest, our breath white in the flashlight beams as we sat breathing hard.

I had been home from Germany four days, and while I was gone I had decided to quit hunting. Two years of knowing that I would probably be drafted and sent to Vietnam, hearing the older Germans talk about World War II, and every day preaching the gospel of Christ changed me. I felt guilty because of all the rabbits, pheasants, ducks, geese, and deer I had killed, which were beautiful and had a right to live. All things had been created spiritually before they were physically. Our family ate the meat, but we didn't need it. We weren't pioneers or Indians, and we were commanded to eat meat mostly in time of famine anyway,

18

and then with thanksgiving. The deer herds had to be controlled, but I knew that I hunted because I liked to kill, not because I was a conservationist. A mule-deer buck was a beautiful animal, sleek and grey, powerful, had a being all its own. To kill was to deny the influence of the Holy Ghost, which I wanted to continue to develop.

I had started three letters to my father to tell him how I had changed, but I couldn't make them sound right, and I knew that I would have to wait until I got home to tell him. I had three older married sisters but no brothers, and my father and I had been very close. Even before I was old enough to buy a license for anything or even shoot, he took me hunting. He helped me make my bows and arrows, bought me a BB-gun, my Browning .22, and my Winchester .270. For my birthdays and Christmases he always gave me something for hunting, although I had bought my own knife when I was eight. We built a walnut gun cabinet, a duck boat, and we cleaned and repaired the camping equipment together every year. Every month we read and talked about the stories in *Outdoor Life* and *Field and Stream*, which I saved.

We had even planned my mission so that I would have the deer hunt to look forward to when I got home. When I met my family at the Salt Lake airport, all my father could talk about driving home to Provo was the opening day Saturday and how wonderful it was having me home again to be with him in the deer camp. Upstairs in my room I found my .270, knife, full cartridge belt, and red hunting clothes laid out on my bed. My father had bought me a new red hat, cleaned and oiled my .270, and loaded three boxes of shells for me to use for target practicing. When I went back

19

downstairs he took me out to see the new sets of antlers he had nailed to the back of the garage the two seasons I was away.

I knew then that I would have to hunt the opening day. I couldn't disappoint my father. We could have Friday night in camp together, and all day Saturday I would drive the draws, help clean the bucks if I had to, pack them on the horses, but I wouldn't kill a buck myself. I would shoot just to stop questions if a buck jumped up and a member of the camp was standing where he could see me, but I would miss. We always came home Saturday night to go to church on Sunday, and I would tell my father Sunday about my decision. I wouldn't hunt during the week or next Saturday, which was the last Saturday. My mother always said that my father should have been born an Indian two hundred years ago so that he could have hunted elk, wolves, buffalo, and grizzly bear, hunted every day.

Climbing up the trail I was the last in line. Ahead of me the flashlights lit up the high oak brush on both sides and the horses' hooves clicked against the rocks. Doc, Bliss, and my father stayed on the horses when we stopped to rest. Because we knew the ridge, organized our drives, and hunted hard, we always got bucks. A camp needed horses to haul the bucks off the high ridge, so we had little competition. Sitting on the edge of the trail, the sweat cooling on my back, I picked up little white pebbles, flipped them away, thought about Germany.

Although I had sold more Books of Mormon than any other elder in the mission and been assistant to President Wunderlich my last five months, I had baptized only two converts in two years. The younger Germans weren't interested in the gospel, and when the older Germans invited me and my companion in, they often talked about the war. They showed us pictures of their sons that we had killed, and they wanted to know why the American army hadn't joined the German army to fight the Russians. They showed us pictures of whole families of relatives burned alive or buried in the rubble during the great Allied bombing raids on Nuremberg, Hamburg, and Dresden. They called Hitler a madman and asked why the English and French governments didn't stop him before 1939. They wanted to know how there could be a God if he let such terrible things happen, and I told them that it wasn't God that caused wars but men. If all mankind would just live the gospel of Christ there wouldn't be any more wars. I wanted to get a doctorate in sociology so that I could teach at B.Y.U. and help people to live together in peace and harmony.

On the streets in the German towns, older men who had been invalided in the war wore yellow armbands with black circles, a lot of them amputees, but there were no beggars. My first fall in Germany, a German brother took me and my companion on a Saturday out to visit a small German military cemetery near Offenbach. One of the caretakers raking leaves under the oak trees said that most of the soldiers had been killed fighting Americans. I picked up a handful of the leaves. In Utah in the fall I had followed wounded bucks by their blood trails on the leaves under the oak brush. In the places where they lay down, the blood soaked slowly into the pressed leaves.

The trail led onto a little flat, and above us the ridge was still black under the stars. In every direction were ridges, canyons, mountains, but they were still black

21

and indistinct. Points of light flashed where hunters climbed other ridges, and in the bottom of Blind Canyon fires still burned. As a boy at night I dreamed about the ridge. Although a lot of big bucks hid in the short, steep, pine-filled draws on the north slope, I liked the south draws best because I could see the bucks running up through the oak brush, shoot for three and four hundred yards if I were on a good ledge. In my dreams I shot and shot, killed the running bucks, their antlers flashing in the sun like swords, rolled them back down the steep side of the draw. And I dreamed too that we jumped five and six bucks in one bunch, and it was like a battle with all of us shooting, but because we gang-hunted I wanted to fill all of the permits myself. I wanted to feel all of the thrill, cut the throats, the blood spreading out through the leaves, holler up to the others how big the bucks were, how many points on the antlers. If we shot too many bucks, on the way down Blind Canyon going home we always gave the smaller ones to other camps, didn't waste any. One opening day I shot three bucks, but they were all singles.

When we stopped on the trail again to rest, Jerry leaned forward to pour some dextrose tablets into my palm. "Quick energy, Troy," he said. "It takes a while for you returned missionaries to get back into shape." Chewing two, I sat and held my .270 between my legs, the barrel cold against the side of my neck, rubbed the stock with the flat of my hand. Up the trail one of the horses stomped.

A Winchester Model 70 mounted with a 3-9x variable scope, the .270 was a present from my father on my sixteenth birthday. The evening I got it, in the sitting position on my bed, left arm tight in the sling, I aimed at the pictures of bears, lions, and deer on my walls, and later out the windows at cars and people passing below on our street, centered the cross hairs. Then I broke the .270 down, oiled each metal part, reassembled it, broke it down again. And I kept filling the magazine with shells, worked the bolt over and over to flip them out on my bed. That night after I showered I got the .270 out of the case again to hold it against my body. I had a .22 pistol, .22 rifle, .22-250 varminter, two shotguns, but my .270 had always been my favorite gun. I had waited for it, knew that my father would give me a deer rifle too when I was sixteen, which was the first year I could buy a buck permit. I liked to take my .270 out of our gun cabinet just to hold it and work the action, wipe it clean with an oiled cloth.

I thought of my guns when I saw the filled-in shrapnel and bullet holes in the old stone German buildings that hadn't been destroyed. If the older German sisters talked long enough about the war, they always cried, and I never asked them about the concentration camps, the SS, or the Gestapo. On a street in Darmstadt after I was transferred from Offenbach, I saw a legless, armless blind man sitting on a padded box singing while another man played a guitar, but there was no cup or dish in front of them and they weren't begging. Some of the older Germans said that they were sorry for the young Americans in Vietnam and asked if my companion and I would have to go too. I knew that if I couldn't get a student defer-ment and go back to B.Y.U. to start my sophomore year, I would be drafted. It was impossible to get into the Utah National Guard. I would kill other men, shoot them in the jungle or running across the rice paddies, their blood turning the brown water near their bodies red. And I knew also by then that the excitement of killing a man must be a little like that of killing a buck.

When we got to the top of the ridge we sat and watched the band of white light grow over the east mountains, our red hats, sweat shirts, and jackets almost black in the half-light. Excited, my heart pounding hard even though I was rested, I pulled the cold shells from my belt to load the .270, heard around me shells clicking into magazines. "Good luck, son," my father said when we stood up, shook my hand. "I hope you nail a big one first thing." The others came over to shake my hand and tell me how good it was to have me back on the ridge again. Separating, we spread out along the top of the ridge to take the points we had drawn Friday night.

Ten minutes later, cradling the .270, I stood on my ledge in the half-light looking down into the pine-filled basin at the head of Sheep Draw on the north side of the ridge. Trembling a little, my mouth dry, I watched the clearings for movement. The light grew and the first shots came booming along the ridge. Then below me two does and a little two-point buck stepped out of the pines into a patch of brush. My body tight, blood pounding in my throat, I slowly raised the .270 and centered the cross hairs over the little buck's heart. I fought the desire to ease down into the sitting position, tighten into the sling, squeeze the trigger slowly. I wanted to hear the explosion, feel the .270 kick, see the little two-point hump and drop, feel that satisfaction again. The first season I carried the .270, I had killed a two-point at first light, had been unable to wait for the bigger buck I wanted. Fighting that feeling, I closed my eyes, opened them. Suddenly the three deer tensed, then crossed the clearing and slipped back into the pines as quiet and smooth as gliding birds. Glad I hadn't shot, I lowered the .270.

At 9 o'clock the camp met to drive Porcupine, the first draw on the west end of the south slope, where we always started. Jerry had passed up a small two-point, and Dean missed three shots at a big buck some hunters had pushed up from below. While Doc and Jerry tested the walkie-talkies again, I scoped the draw and the basin. Broken only by ledges and scattered pines, the leafless oak brush and scrub maple were like a smooth low-lying haze. But a dozen bucks could be hiding, waiting. You never knew. Each draw was a surprise. Everything would be quiet, not even a bird moving, then two or three bucks would be running in front of the line, running grey and beautiful, heads up, antlers gleaming in the sun, going for the top and the thick pines on the north slope, and then the shooting would start. It was as if you had waited all year for just that one moment because it was the best time out of the whole year.

I stopped the scope on a patch of scrub maple where I had killed a three-point the season before I left to go on my mission. To the left was the clearing where Jerry had killed the biggest buck ever killed on the ridge, a big eight-point with a forty-inch spread. He had the mounted head in his real estate office. I knew where all of the big bucks had been killed. We cut the legs off the bucks at the knee to load them on the horses, and sometimes I found legs from two and three seasons back. There was always a black stain on the ground where the entrails had lain the year before. In twenty-five years the camp had killed over a hundred and fifty bucks on the ridge.

"Okay," Doc said, "let's get the big ones. There's one down in there for you, Troy, a nice big four-point." The clear sky was dark blue, and now the warming sun brought out the dusty smell of brush and dead leaves. Lines of blue ridges and mountains extended to the horizon on every side.

Doc and my father stayed on the rim, and Jerry led the rest of us down into the draw to organize the drive, Bliss riding his horse. We formed the line, each of us a hundred yards apart across the bottom and up both sides, and started slowly back toward the top. Expecting to see a big buck jump up any minute, excited but controlling myself, I walked tense, stopped, checked the openings ahead on both sides, listened for deer running through the brush. Across the draw, Dean and Ken vanished, reappeared, stopped to throw rocks ahead of them, their red hunting clothes bright against the grey leafless brush. Jerry and Bliss were above me where I couldn't see them. I stopped to toe the fresh droppings with my boot, knelt on one knee to look at the fresh tracks in the deer trail I was on. Mouth dry, hands sweaty on the .270, I froze when Ken first jumped seven does and fawns, which I scoped until they vanished over the top, their white rear ends flashing. Shooting echoed from ridge to ridge, some of it coming in sharp bursts like machine-gun fire, and far down the draw four hunters stood together on a knoll. When I was a boy, the shooting from the other ridges always made me jealous.

I had just walked out onto a ledge at the bottom end of the basin topping the draw when Dean yelled, "Buck! Buck! Buck! He's in the bottom!" Dean shot twice, shot again. Warned, my heart pounding in my throat, I half raised the .270. Another rifle started. Then I saw the big buck moving through the high scrub maples, head down, going smooth like a cat, not making the big ten-foot bounding jumps. But when I jammed the .270 into my shoulder, got the cross hairs on him, he was already blundering, crashing into the brush. A round patch of blood widened behind the shoulder on the grey side, and his mouth dripped blood. Lung-shot. Hit again, he came crashing, rolling back down toward the bottom. He got up, shook his head. Hit again, he humped and dropped, lay in a clearing. The whooping started then, and Dean, Ken following him, jogged down through the brush, hollered for directions twice. They hollered up that he was a fat four-point, cut his throat, then got out their cameras to take colored slides before they cleaned him. Breathing deep, I tried to stop trembling.

"Aren't you coming down, Troy?" Bliss asked me when he came past leading his horse through the brush.

"No, I'll stay here. They don't need me."

"I shot but I think Dean got him, unless you did."

"No, I didn't."

"Too bad, looks like a nice buck. Jerry's going to stay put and watch for anything pushed up from the bottom by the other camps."

I sat down on the ledge, laid the .270 on my hat and ate a Hershey bar, rinsed my teeth and drank from my canteen. Dean, Ken, and Bliss bent over the buck. Watching two hawks circle out over the draw, I picked up a dead branch, broke off pieces and flipped them away.

Before I was sixteen and could shoot a buck, using my own knife I cut the throats of my father's bucks and

27

other bucks I got to first. My father taught me how to clean a buck, cut around the genitals, up through the stomach and ribs, reach up into the chest and grab the severed wind pipe to pull everything out together without getting my hands bloody above the wrists. I always cut the heart away from the blue pile of entrails to hold up and see if it had been hit. Afterward my father poured water on my hands from his canteen and I wiped them clean with handfuls of dry leaves. Yet even with two or three of us shooting, hit several times, a buck still might not go down. A buck with both front legs shot off would still lunge forward, work his antlers through the low limbs, crawl to get away. Following blood trails, I had found pieces of entrails snagged on the oak brush and splinters of bone lying on the leaves.

The limbless blind man made me think about the fantastic pain I caused by just squeezing the trigger of my .270 to send the hundred-and-fifty-grain slug at three thousand feet per second slamming into a buck. I saw him once more before President Wunderlich made me a zone leader and transferred me from Darmstadt to Heidelberg. He rode in a big rucksack on his friend's back, just his head showing, bobbing, as if he saw the passing people and into the store windows. His friend carried the guitar and the padded box. When I ate, dressed, showered, I wondered how he did those things. Lying in bed at night I tried to imagine what it would be like for him to be in bed, and I wanted to know if he was married. I knew then that I couldn't go on hunting and killing when I got home and still expect to feel the full influence of the Holy Ghost in my life, be spiritual, which had to be earned. Breaking off the last few pieces of the dead branch, I flipped them over the ledge. Then I got out my clean handkerchief and wiped off the scope and the .270.

Ken, Dean, and Bliss loaded the buck on the horse and we hunted the basin to the top of the ridge, where they hung the buck from the low limb of a big pine. In Middle Draw, the last drive we always made before lunch and the draw where I had killed the two-point when I was sixteen, Doc and my father both shot three-points as they came up out of the basin over the top. I didn't see either buck, but stood cradling the .270, counted the shots, felt empty, then heard Jerry hollering after he talked to Doc on the walkie-talkie. When we got to the top we helped drag the bucks over to the trail to hang them up. I broke sticks to prop open the stomachs so the bucks would cool faster. We always hung our bucks in the garage to cure for a week before we had them cut up for the freezer. Skinned, the heads cut off, they hung stiff and white upside down, the blunt front legs sticking out, spots of blood on the cement floor.

"Well, Troy," my father said when we all gathered to eat lunch on the ledge above Doc's draw, "I wish that you had been on the rim instead of me. Those two three-points came sneaking up through the brush ahead of you boys in the line just perfect. It couldn't have been prettier."

"No, I guess not," I said. Ken, Jerry, and Dean had black dry deer blood on their red sweat shirts and blue Levis. You couldn't wash the smell of the blood from your hands unless you had hot soap and water, but you could get the blood out from under your fingernails with the point of a sharp hunting knife.

"Oh, we'll get Troy a nice buck today or next Saturday, don't worry about that," Doc said. Doc and

Bliss had taken the bridles off the horses and poured some oats for them.

"Sure," Jerry said, unwrapping a piece of cake.

Eating my sandwich, I looked out over the draw toward the lines of blue ridges out past Blind Canyon. Doc had killed three bucks one opening day in the basin as they ran past him at seventy-five yards; after that everybody in camp called it Doc's Draw. Each line of ridges was a different shade of blue. All the shooting had stopped. I was glad that my father had Doc and Bliss to hunt with. They had worked on the Union Pacific together for thirty years. My father had never been on a mission. He had written me long letters about the duck, pheasant, and deer hunts and sent me the best colored slides he had taken. Every month he mailed me his copies of *Outdoor Life* and *Field and Stream*. When I was a boy and my mother made me turn off my bedroom light, I used a flashlight to reread my favorite hunting stories by.

After we ate lunch, the others got their red jackets from the saddlebags to use for pillows, pulled their red hats down over their eyes and lay back on the ledge to doze in the warm sun. Below me nothing moved in the draw. I picked up white chips of rock and flipped them over the ledge. Although I wouldn't hunt I planned to do a lot of back-packing, learn the names of all the Rocky Mountain flora and fauna, and at night study the stars. When I got married and had sons, I wanted them to see the real beauty, design, and completeness of Nature, which God had created. I wanted to be as close to my sons as my father had been to me, but without guns and killing. I wouldn't let them carry .22s or varmint rifles to kill the hawks, rabbits, rock chucks, and squirrels they saw, as my father had let

30

me. I wanted them to understand the pioneers and Indians, but they didn't have to hunt to do that. We could start an arrowhead collection and visit all of the historical spots in the state.

A chipmunk came up over the face of the ledge, found a piece of bread. With the shooting stopped, it was very quiet. I flipped a chip of rock. I had read an article by one of the apostles who had visited the Mormon servicemen in Vietnam. He said that in one meeting the men came to the tent carrying their rifles. In the prayers they prayed for the Mormon boys killed the week before, prayed for the spirit of the Lord for themselves. After the testimony meeting some of the soldiers told the apostle that they had met him as missionaries in Europe nine months before when he was touring the missions. In the German magazines I saw pictures of American wounded being carried to helicopters on stretchers, medics running alongside with lifted plasma bottles. Wrapped in their ponchos the American dead lay in rows like packages, but the Viet Cong dead were never covered. I flipped another piece of rock and the chipmunk vanished back over the face of the ledge.

Before we dropped down into Doc's Draw, three hunters on horses from another camp came along the ridge trail. They wanted to know where we got the three nice bucks we had hanging up. "They don't organize and they don't know the country, so all they get are spikes and two-points," Doc said after they left. "They might as well stay in camp as come up on this ridge and ride around."

We jumped one bunch of six does and fawns at the lower end of Doc's Draw, and in the basin Ken, who was across from me, shot a big four-point. Hollering, he directed me to him in the thick brush. One antler dug through the dead leaves into the black dirt, the big buck lay on his side, the four points on each side of the antlers white-tipped, the blood bright red on the leaves. Standing there, I wondered if I had scared the buck out to Ken. I didn't pull his head downhill to cut his throat. He was still perfect, the eyes not yet glazed. He still seemed alive, still had that beautiful grey live symmetry as if he might suddenly jump and run. Bending, I ran my hand over the hard antlers, along the neck and onto the heavy shoulders. When Ken and Dean broke through the brush, I told them that I would go and show Bliss the best way to bring the horse down.

"Okay," Ken said. He leaned his rifle against a rock and got out his camera.

"Looks like you really busted a nice one, Ken," Dean said. "Good work."

"Finally."

Climbing up through the brush, I heard them talking. I had actually prayed for a big four-point like Ken's the first morning I had carried the new .270. My father beside me on the ledge overlooking the basin at the top of middle draw, I gripped the Winchester, whispered the prayer to myself, and I would have knelt down too if I had thought that it would do any good. But when in the first light I saw the little two-point standing in the patch of sagebrush with a doe, I moved into the sitting position, tightened into the sling, and killed him with a perfect heart shot, started then to run. When my father got down to me and the little buck, he put his rifle down and hugged me. I cleaned the buck, holding up his shattered heart in my hand to look for pieces of the slug. I had killed a lot of pheasants, ducks, geese, and rabbits before I was sixteen, but I had never felt like that. My father nailed the two-point's antlers over the garage door next to the biggest spread of antlers he had ever taken.

At 2 o'clock we crossed from the south slope of the ridge to the north to hunt the smaller steeper draws full of thick pines. It was cooler there than on the south slope. We jumped bucks, but they were hard to hit running through the pines, and they all got away over the top past Doc and my father. Because the bucks liked to hide in the pines, there was a lot of sign on the deer trails. I saw a beautiful little spike, but didn't even raise the .270 to put the scope on him, just watched him until he moved. It made me happy just to watch him. Other years I had found blood trails in the pines from the deer wounded lower on the ridge that sneaked up in the thick cover to die. The second year the scattered bones were white, with hair left only on the legs and skull.

In the next basin, ahead of the others, I sat down against a pine. I cut a Baby Ruth bar in sections with my knife, drank from my canteen, rinsed my teeth, the air cool against my face and throat. Taking off my heavy cartridge belt, I laid it across my knees, began to line the shells up in the loops so that they were all exactly even. I pulled one out and fingered it. The hundred-and-fifty-grain slug with the lead tip and core was built to explode on contact with bone or heavy muscle. In junior high school every fall I took some of my father's shells with me to class so that I could put my hand in my pocket and feel them. I took my hunting knife one day, but my home-room teacher picked it up and kept it in her desk until school was out in the afternoon. After my father gave me the .270 for my birthday, I loaded my empty brass on his reloading outfit. At night I poured three or four boxes of shells onto my bed just to run my fingers through them. Alone, I dressed in my red hat and shirt, wore my knife and full cartridge belt, cradled the .270 in my left arm to look at myself in the mirror.

Below me in the pines a small bird lit on a dead branch. Everything was in shadow. The German forests seemed always to be in shadow, as if the season were always winter but without snow. The .270 shell I had taken out of the belt was heavy in my palm. One Saturday afternoon a week before President Wunderlich called me to Frankfurt as his assistant, my companion and I rode our bicycles out into the woods near Heidelberg to an area where a German brother said there had been fighting. We walked through the trees until we came to the top of a hill dotted with shallow pits, which I knew must be old shell holes. Some of the pines looked as if they had been hit by lightning a long time ago. Scratching with a stick, my companion found an American hand-grenade pin and three empty rifle shells so corroded that he had to scrape them on a rock to tell if they were American or German. He offered me one of the shells, but I told him no. When we got back to our room he put his find in a little box to save and take home. Placing the .270 shell back in the belt loop, I took out my handkerchief and wiped off the scope and the rifle.

At 4 o'clock Jerry organized the drive for West Draw. It was the last drive before we went down the ridge to break camp and start the long trip out of Blind Canyon and back to Provo. The shooting from the other ridges had stopped again. The lines of ridges were darker blue now, some of the ledges white like patches of early snow. The Ute Indians buried their dead high in the canyons in the ledges, but I had never found one of the rock-piled graves. I had always wondered if the Indians had hunted the high ridges too or whether they found enough game lower down. As we stood together at the top of the draw, in the afternoon light the hats and sweat shirts seemed darker red. I was glad it was the last drive and we were going home.

Because Jerry wanted to take me out of the line and put me on a point above an opening in the pines called the bowl, Doc held out his walkie-talkie to me. The bowl was the best spot in the basin at the head of West Draw. "No," I said, "I'll go down in the pines and help make the drive. You take the bowl, Bliss; you haven't filled your permit yet."

"Now, Troy," Doc said, "you've hunted hard in that line all day without any luck, and this is your last chance until next Saturday, unless you and your dad get out during the week for a little afternoon hunting. We'd all like to see you get a nice buck."

"No. I don't want to do that."

"Go ahead, Troy," Jerry said. "We all got nice bucks the last two seasons. We're not sweating it."

"Oh no."

"Go on, son," my father said, and Doc put the walkie-talkie into my hand.

"Sure," Jerry said, gripping my shoulder.

Ten minutes later I climbed up to the ledge to the left and nearly to the top of the bowl and sat down. The oak brush was all knee high, stunted, and fallen leaves covered the rocks and bare spots. Because of the timber, none of the others could see me, so I wouldn't even have to shoot if a buck came up through the bowl. I had never killed a buck in West Draw. Sitting

35

there, cradling the .270, I thought about Sunday morning and meeting everybody in church after two years away. I was anxious to tell about all the things that I had learned while I was in Germany on my mission, tell of my experiences, and I wanted to bear my testimony of the truthfulness of the gospel of Christ. I breathed in the cool air full of the smell of pines.

"You ready, Troy?"

I raised the walkie-talkie. "Yes."

"Keep your eyes open. There's an awful lot of tracks and droppings down here on these trails."

Picking up a handful of the wind-blown oak leaves caught in a crack in the ledge, I let them sift through my fingers. Perhaps my father and I could find something else we liked to do together. One of the reasons I wanted to get my doctorate in sociology and teach at B.Y.U. was so that I could live in Provo and raise my family there after I got married. Because my father had given me my .270 for my sixteenth birthday, I would always keep it, but I would get rid of my other guns and my eight-year collection of *Field and Stream* and *Outdoor Life*. I didn't want my sons to get started on them. "Keep your eyes open, Troy. Something moving out ahead." I reached down and clicked off the walkie-talkie. Nobody shot. Nothing moved. I waited. Then right at the bottom edge of the bowl a buck stepped out of the pines. Chest tightening, I slowly lifted the .270 to bring the scope to my eye. A nice three-point. Another buck stepped out, another three-point, moved up to the first. Heart slamming, I scoped them both, when two more moved out of the pines at the same place. They were both four-points, the last one a beautiful big buck with a wide heavy set of antlers.

Bent forward, breathing deep, the blood beginning to pound in my ears, I held the scope to my eye. They were beautiful. I just wanted to watch them, prayed nobody would make it to the edge of the pines in time for a shot. The bucks stopped to look back, started moving again, the big buck leading now. Slipping my arm into the sling, I got into the sitting position to steady my scope. The bucks were nervous but still walking. Beautiful. Biting my lower lip, I shifted the cross hairs back up to the big buck. The antlers were perfectly matched on each side. My pounding blood sounded like rushing water in my ears, louder and louder. Beautiful. I closed my eyes against the feeling, gripped harder, breathless.

The .270 slammed my shoulder, the explosion part of my feeling. Heart-shot, the big buck humped and went down. The other bucks ran now in high leaping bounds, instinct driving them toward the top and me. I shot over the leader, adjusted, got him through the back at seventy-five yards, and he went smashing down. I shot at the first three-point as he came level with me, missed twice. Kneeling, I crammed in more shells, cursed, slammed the bolt home, held the cross hairs on him, saw him come rolling back down the slope. Alone, the last buck was nearly to the top. I shot, missed, stood up, spun him around with a hit in the front leg, got him just as he topped the skyline. He came crashing end-over-end back down the steep slope into the bowl. I found the raised head of the back-shot buck in the scope, shot, and everything was quiet.

"Oh no, no, no," I said, "oh no." Grabbing the short oak brush with my free hand when I slipped, I angled across to the last buck. "No," I said, "no." I laid the .270 down to pull the buck around so that his head was down-hill, then cut his throat. I had to shoot the second buck again to kill him. Whooping and yelling, somebody was climbing toward me up through the brush. "Oh no," I said. I cut the big four-point's throat last, my knife and hands red with blood, his antlers thick at the base where I grabbed them with my sticky hands. "No, no." Still trembling, I knelt down by the big buck's head. His pooled blood started to trickle down through the oak leaves. "Oh, Jesus, Jesus," I whispered.

THE RABBIT HUNT

When Allen got back to his bedroom after brushing his teeth, he opened his gun cabinet and took out five boxes of shells and his Browning .22 automatic rifle. It was Saturday. In twenty minutes he was supposed to be at the chapel to pick up the boys from his Sunday School class for a rabbit hunt. The hunt was a reward for the boys' being quiet during July (the girls were always quiet). And he knew that if he were ten minutes late they would be potting the pigeons off the chapel roof. But they were pretty good kids, and they should all have a good time, although it would be hot. He planned to go on his mission in September, so this would be the last real outing. He had enjoyed teaching the class while he'd been going to school. He had finished his first year of pre-dent.

The snake-bite kit! It was too hot for rattlesnakes in the open sagebrush during the day, but there was always some chance, at least around rocks. His father had warned him again at breakfast about the deep gullies, particularly in Dog Valley. Because the sage always grew right to the edge of the sheer clay sides, an excited kid chasing a wounded rabbit could take a twenty-foot dive into one. Wouldn't that be jolly. Each of the kids had gone through the required state gun-safety course. All he and Larry needed to do was to keep them in some kind of line and out of the high sage. The mothers had all given their permission.

Allen unbuttoned his faded Levis and pulled his white T-shirt tight across his stomach, then buttoned up again and combed his hair. Because Cathy liked his hair sun-bleached, he wasn't wearing a hat. He winked at her picture. They had a date at seven. His summer construction job paid well, kept him in great shape—and he had Cathy, which made for a big summer so far. He picked up the Browning and shells, then stood to bow his head and say a short prayer. Buzzing, a big yellow hornet bumped at the window screen.

Going down the hall he banged on Danny's door. "Hey, Mom said to get up!" Danny groaned. "Come on, kid, it's Saturday morning. Hit the deck." Danny hunted everything with him and his father—ducks, geese, pheasants, rabbits, deer—but he had a special piano lesson for his recital, so he couldn't make it this time. Coming down the stairs and into the kitchen, Allen heard his mother on the back porch talking to Mrs. Miller. His father had left for the office. He got his canteen, moved some of the breakfast dishes aside to fill it at the sink and then took his lunch out of the refrigerator.

"Good morning, Mrs. Miller," he said when he got on the porch.

She greeted him and she and his mother went on talking. He smashed two flies trapped against the inside of his windshield and then had to clean the glass with a Kleenex. One thing he didn't like about hunting in August was the flies. The boys would have to keep moving.

When he started his engine, his mother came down the steps. "Have a good time, son, and see that those boys behave themselves."

"I will, Mom." She squeezed his arm, then waved as he backed out. Behind her over the garage door hung the antlers from a dozen deer hunts, some of them bleached white. He and his father always nailed up the biggest antlers each fall.

He waved back at his mother, shifted to drive and moved down the quiet street. Danny would have the yard work to do alone. Mrs. Wayne stopped her raking to wave. She hadn't always been *quite* that friendly. When he was a boy she used to chase him off for sniping birds out of her big trees with his BB gun. But he never shot songbirds (none of the kids did), just starlings and sparrows.

The boys saw him when he crossed Third South. Dressed in cut-offs, carrying sack lunches and guns, they came charging off the church lawn, whooping, excited, their white T-shirts and naked legs flashing in the new sunlight. He made them put all of the guns in the trunk on the old blanket. They groaned. They wanted to hold their guns, said they would be careful. "Not on your life," he said. He made sure each action was open before he laid the guns on the old blanket.

Larry drove up. They gathered in a circle for prayer, then left, driving south on 91 toward Levan. They would hunt near Levan first, then drive farther west to Dog Valley at the base of Battle Mountain, where the best hunting was. The boys wanted to look for arrowheads and bones at the mountain, until he told

41

them that there had been no massacre.

Larry right on his tail, they made Nephi in less than an hour, even though they had to stop once to get a hornet out of the car. The valley grew wider and more barren. Except for the black pinyon pines on the low, rounded mountains and squares of dry-land wheat on the flats, sagebrush covered everything. Patches of fur showed where cars had pounded jack rabbits into the asphalt, and every mile or two a hawk sat perched on top of a power pole.

Speaking over the rush of warm air, the boys told hunting stories. Allen told them about the time he and two friends had killed two hundred jack rabbits on a single overnight hunt. They used a spotlight to blind the rabbits along the old roads, and he still had the sugar sack full of tails somewhere. The boys already had a tail contest set up. Later, when those in the back seat started to tell dirty jokes, their voices muffled, he had to tell them to knock it off. "This is still a Sunday School class," he said. Embarrassed, they quieted down. They were good kids, a little rowdy at times, but still basically good kids. They liked him because he had played high school ball.

"Hey look," Bruce hollered, "pheasants!"

Allen caught just a glimpse of the small flock in the corner of a cut wheat field. Two roosters. The boys wanted to know when the season opened. Judas, how he liked to walk through the corn, kick up the big roosters, and then blast them down in long trails of bright feathers. Last year for the first time in his life he had made a triple, jumped three roosters simultaneously out of one weed clump and killed all three. His father walked clear across the field to slap him on the back and shake his hand. One of the things he'd miss most on his mission was hunting.

At Levan (UNINCORPORATED, POPULATION 247), Allen turned off onto the dirt road and drove across the sage flats toward the mountains and the power line. With Larry half a mile behind him in the dust, Allen pulled off at the usual place. While he waited for Larry, the kids mined two of the big ant hills with cherry bombs, exploding them in sudden bursts of dust. But already they brushed at the flies. "Okay, *brethren*, gather over here," he said finally. They groaned. "Now stay in line, keep out of the high sage, and don't fall into a gully." They laughed." And don't shoot songbirds."

"Ah, Allen, why not?" somebody asked in a phony voice.

They shoved and pushed when he turned to open his trunk. "Just take it easy." As each boy received his gun, Larry spaced him in the line. Allen picked up the Browning and closed the lid. They would follow the power poles to the ledges, where they would trap the rabbits and get the best shooting until Dog Valley. He walked into the space that Larry had left him in the middle. "Okay, load your guns!"

Stepping back away from a hornet that flew by him, Allen dropped the inch-long shells into the tube magazine, then poured the rest of the box into his pocket. T-shirts off, brown backs already gleaming with sweat under the sun, the boys waited, brushed flies. With his light complexion he couldn't take nearly the sun they could. Larry was ready on the north end. Allen raised his arm, and with a ripple of shouts, they started. Directly above his head the power cables crackled and buzzed. The poles would help to keep the line straight. No bad gullies cut between them and the ledges.

Allen walked alert, finger on the safety. He liked the tight sensation, the feel of the Browning. Next to him Ken dropped a sparrow in a puff of feathers. "Come on, Daniel Boone," he said, "we're not after sparrows." Then the shooting started at the south end, but nobody yelled, so he knew that the rabbit got away. Five minutes later Merrill got the first jack, whooped, held it up for everybody to see then dropped it to rip off the tail.

The cracking of the .22s increased as they crowded more rabbits in front of them. But the boys had killed a dozen between them before Allen got his first good shot. The jack crossed close in front of him, ears laid back, really moving. He held the trigger down, read the spurts of dust, both eyes open, the thrill shrinking his guts. A little more lead, then "w-h-a-p," and the jack somersaulted into the dust, squealed. Holding it with his foot, he put the barrel next to its head and pulled the trigger.

"Okay, let's take five!" he yelled. He didn't want anybody dropping from heat exhaustion.

Squatting, they drank from their canteens, loaded their guns, shouted to each other about how many they had killed. The white T-shirts stuffed into their back pockets looked like tails. Allen reloaded. Twice as big as a cat, the dead jack was a soft grey color except for the white tail and underbelly. Already flies buzzed around it, and a big ant crawled in one of the long ears. He reached down and jerked off the tail.

The shooting got better. Pairs of robins and small flocks of bluebirds and larks flew ahead of them. Twice they jumped hawks, and once an owl, but always out of range. A quarter of a mile from the shimmering

44

ledges he called the boys in. "Okay," he said, "we always get a lot of rabbits here, but don't climb up into the ledges." Vaulting the sage clumps and yelling like Comanches, they went back into the line.

Trapped, the rabbits ran back through the line or around the ledges and up the hill. The automatics cracked, the other guns slower, bullets ricocheting, zinging. Five or six rabbits flashed through the sage ahead of Allen, others trying to sneak by. Mouth dry, heart pounding, he shot, loaded and kept shooting, the Browning slick with sweat. Broken-backed, one jack pawed the ground dog-fashion, and he finished it. The line got ragged, the boys shouting now, some cursing. He and Larry yelled them back.

Then Allen got two, one sitting, front legs out like hands. "W-h-a-p!" and it caved in, the head half gone. The second he toppled back over a rock shelf. As they neared the ledges the shooting crescendoed, then suddenly slacked off, the rabbits gone. The boys ran back and forth to head-shoot wounded rabbits, argue over kills, rip tails, count the score. Then they stood there all together, wiping the sweat from their eyes with their shirts, drinking, sorry it was over, laughing.

"Okay, pretty good," Allen said; "we'll rest under that big pinion over there." They could find rabbits higher up, but the pinions and ledges made the hunting too tricky, and there could be snakes.

Sitting in the warm shade, they piled the tails in the little mounds before them, kidded Allen and Larry about not being top guns. With the last of their water they washed down the melted Hershey bars. Allen dampened his handkerchief and wiped the grey dust from his face, neck and arms, then ate an apple to clean his teeth. The black flies they brushed away lit on

45

the little piles of blood-specked tails. A hornet swung back and forth over his feet and legs a dozen times before it flew away. Below them the aluminum-roofed barns glimmered and on the highway windshields flashed the sun.

The big excitement gone now, resting, they talked hunting or smoothed the dirt to play ticktacktoe. They wanted to know more about the big rabbit hunt when he and his friends had killed over two hundred. He gave them all the details. He, Steve, and Kevin had gone on a two-day hunt out in the west desert. They had hunted ducks at Fish Springs during the day and rabbits at night along the road with a spotlight. They got one kit fox.

"Hey, look!"

Allen turned. Below them seventy-five yards, one of the brown hawks had lit on a power pole. Allen watched, then slowly reached for the Browning. "Okay, you jokers, move aside," he said, "and we'll see who's the Daniel Boone around here." He winked at Larry. "We buy the root beers if I miss; you buy us malts if I drop the hawk." Larry laughed.

"Okay," somebody said, "you're on."

Even from the prone it was a long shot with a .22, although with his deer rifle he had killed hawks at four times the range. But, at the crack of the Browning, the hawk fell lazily from the pole. Yelling, T-shirts bobbing, the boys charged down the hill after it. Lon and Bruce, who brought the hawk back, wings spread between them, claimed the talons if Allen didn't want them. Allen held the warm, soft hawk. "Neat," Randy said. With his pocketknife Lon cut off the talons, which he and Bruce hung around their necks with string. The other boys groaned. Danny or Cathy's little brother Bobby would like the talons. The hawk's black eyes still glistened.

Before they left, Allen jacked them up about the swearing he had heard. "Now there's absolutely no need for that," he told them. "What about that lesson we had two weeks ago?" They promised. He had to keep after them. They knew that he was going on a mission. The line of power poles led back to the two cars glimmering in the expanse of grey-green sage, but they would cut north. The sun was hotter.

At first they got shooting, but then it thinned out, as it could sometimes. Bored, the boys shot the pencil-long grey lizards, blew up ant hills with cherry bombs, or shot at the large yellow-winged grasshoppers that flew up to light in front of them. Verlin killed a squirrel. They formed firing squads to kill the sparrows, tried to find three or four in the top of the same dead sage. Twice Allen had to stop the boys next to him from shooting the robins, larks, and bluebirds. They laughed, yelled, "Hey, Allen, can I shoot this beat-up old robin?" Just after he brought them in to cross the one deep gully at a spot he had found, he had to shout at them not to shoot towards the cars. All he or Larry needed was a hole through a windshield.

The boys jumped when their naked backs touched the hot plastic seat covers and sat forward, groaned when Larry drove out first. Five miles west of Levan they pulled off at the grove to eat. An artesian well flowed in the center of the cottonwoods, and out behind was a small sink-fed slough. Allen made them all wash, and they blessed the food. After he ate he rinsed his teeth at the well and combed his hair. The boys grew quiet. Some of them flipped pebbles at the hornets settled near the edge of the water around the well.

47

Hornets liked anything wet. Clean a deer, rabbit, or even a pheasant, and the smell brought hornets if the weather was warm. He told the boys how good the hunting would be in Dog Valley. The last part of the drive was always fantastic, so they should save plenty of shells.

Feeling clean, Allen dozed and came awake to a duck squawking. Twisting and turning, a drake mallard flew from the slough out through the cottonwoods. He watched it disappear. A flock of mallards coming into the decoys was even better than rooster pheasants exploding out of the corn. Heart thudding, he liked to crouch in the blind, wait, then stand suddenly to kill just the green-headed drakes out of the flock. A fly lit near his mouth, tickled; he brushed it away.

By 2 o'clock they were on the road driving west toward Dog Valley. The land was barren, empty, not even fences, only the power line. Then they topped the last rise, and Dog Valley curved off to the northwest in front of them; Battle Mountain, the highest peak in the Tintic Range, was on the far side. The sage clung to the bottom, some of it head-high right at the edge of the deep center gully. He told the boys that the best drive was on the east side coming back. There a deep wash cut into the main gully at right angles to form a trap. Ahead the power line left the road to cut down across the middle of the valley.

The boys asked about deer in the Tintic, and he told them that the biggest rack of antlers nailed on their garage came off Battle Mountain. It was the year before he could legally carry a rifle. His father had made a fantastic three-hundred-yard shot that dumped the big running four-point buck in a crashing tangle down the side of the ravine. Blood up to his elbows, he had cleaned the buck for his father, then washed his hands and arms in the snow. When he got his dental practice going, they would hunt elk in Wyoming and grizzlies in Alaska. Allen braked to turn off the asphalt, and the heat came in through the open windows at them.

Standing next to the car, Allen pulled off his T-shirt and stuffed it into his back pocket. The boys whistled, "Hey look, it's Mr. America," somebody said. They laughed. He got the suntan lotion from his car. When he unlocked the trunk the first thing he saw was the blunt-legged hawk stuffed in between the spare and the jack. David wanted to show it to his mother. "Okay, okay, don't shove, brethren," he said. He had told Larry to leave him the spot next to the gully. It was over twenty feet deep in places, a seep in the bottom, and with all of the good shooting coming up somebody might get careless. He closed the trunk, and then reached down to pinch an ant that crawled through the hair just above his sock.

They got better shooting than at Levan, but it wasn't so fast that the boys didn't take time to pot sparrows and lizards. Just after they crossed under the power line Randy shot a big blow snake. He screamed rattler, jumped back and started shooting, and everybody went charging over to where he was. Allen ran. He had warned them twice about snakes. The blow snake lay tangling itself, white-bellied against the yellow and black, shot through the body half a dozen times from four guns and not dead yet. "Better be careful your *rattlesnake* doesn't bite you, Randy," he said. They all laughed, but they were disappointed it wasn't a rattler.

Twice Allen ducked into the high sage to find a

spot to cross the center gully. They crossed at three-thirty. While the kids formed the new line, he stood at the gully's edge and watched the hornets around the stagnant puddles in the bottom. One flew up and kept circling his head; he didn't wave it away, and it flew back down to the water.

Tired, the boys began to drag a little, but then Merrill gut-shot a pregnant rabbit and that brought them back to life. Some of the boys shot at the hawks that circled, riding the hot afternoon thermals. Hunting the trap where the wash hit the gully would be an excellent way to end the hunt, which the boys would appreciate. His father always said that it was the best spot in the state.

When they had hunted back to where the power poles crossed the valley, Allen signaled a halt. "Okay, take five!" He wanted them to rest before the last drive. Those who had water shared it, which he liked to see, and then they sat brushing at the flies, their front pockets bulging with tails. By the time they counted the tails, stopped in Nephi for drinks (they would get their root beers anyway), and had the prayer at the church, it would be after six before he got home. Thirty feet in front of him three robins lit in the top of a dead sage.

Allen stood up. A mile farther on the two cars glimmered at the edge of the road. It had been a good day, but it would be nice to get home, shower, dress in cool clean clothes, and go over to Cathy's. Maybe they would watch TV—wait for her brother Bobby to get lost. Sunday was always a good day too, quiet, with church, dinner, and then in the evening homemade ice cream out on the patio with Cathy and the family. After that maybe just a walk down the sidewalk under the trees. He knew that Cathy would wait for him while he was on his mission if he asked her to.

Behind him they talked about the pregnant rabbit, some of the older boys whispering, snickering. Suddenly there was a ragged "c-r-a-c-k!" One robin flew from the top of the dead sage; two dropped in puffs of brown-white feathers. "Ah, one got away. You guys are a bum firing squad." Allen turned. Lon, Bruce, and Phil stood holding their raised .22s, David beside them. It had been David's voice.

"Now what did you do that for?"

"Ah, Allen, they're just birds."

Lon and Bruce still wore the hawk talons, the string dirty now. All four smiled. He looked at them, then slowly shook his head, started to grin. What was the use. "Okay, okay, okay," he said, "just forget *all* about what I told you. But I'll be very glad to get you home to the care and keeping of your mothers." They laughed.

Across the valley a big stake-bed cattle truck kicked up a plume of dust at the base of Battle Mountain. Reaching down, Allen took the Browning from against the sage where he had leaned it. "All right," he said, "let's get back into line. This is the big one." Rested, eager again, they trotted back to their positions, T-shirts bobbing. "Take it easy!" he hollered. Above him the power cables sizzled and popped, the tall poles extending across and down the valley to infinity. He waved to Larry.

The shooting began slowly, grew, became a steady crackle; the boys started then to yell. They went on. Rabbits flashed through the sage everywhere, ten or twelve breaking into the open at one time, running back from the walls of the wash, trying for the hill.

51

Rabbits dropped or went somersaulting. Wounded, spurts of dust jumping around it, one rabbit ran in a tight circle. Rabbits squealed. Excited, yelling, cursing, leaping over the sage, the crackle of their guns growing, the boys broke from line, whirling to shoot to the side or back, anywhere. Caught in a spur of sage, Allen saw it happening. Larry was waving, shouting something.

Running now because he had to stop the boys, scared, Allen got just to the edge of the high stuff when he heard the clip, clip, clip of the slugs from an automatic cutting the sage in front of him. He felt something hit him twice, like slaps. His legs went weak, he stumbled, dropped the Browning, and fell forward, hitting on his right shoulder in a small clearing. Dazed, he lay on his side facing the sun. He looked down at the two little black holes in his naked stomach and chest. They didn't bleed. Cheek against the dirt, he saw the dusty Browning, the pebbles and twigs.

Then very gradually the pain began, became finally hot coals, spilt acid, knives pushed into him, and beyond all he had ever believed pain was or could be. Amazed, he curled, wrapped his arms around, squeezed, trying to stop the pain. Then he saw only a white glare. He couldn't tell if he had limbs, arms and legs, the pain blotting out all feeling except pain. There was a center to the pain, an intensity, which seemed beyond feeling, only void. And he wanted to stop the pain, squeeze harder, and curse, scream, but he couldn't make any sound.

Slowly the pain faded, almost like noise, and he felt his body relax, his arms. Then a hornet swung back and forth over his feet, above his hands, over his face. It lit on his cheek under his eye. But he couldn't raise his hand to brush it away. He couldn't feel it. Someone stood over him blocking out the sun, knelt down. He couldn't open his mouth to speak, tell them what to do, get to a telephone and call his folks. He couldn't hear anything. A blurred face vanished in the weak yellow glow. He began to choke and gasp against the blood filling his throat and mouth. And then he couldn't see.

THE CLINIC

Steve pulled open the heavy glass door to the clinic, walked in, stopped, took off his sunglasses, and rubbed the burning spots behind both ears. The army doctor had told him that rubbing or scratching his skin could cause infection. The clinic smell was still the same. He had his five senses, but he needed to feel the old emotions, or at least recall them. Dr. Jensen had taken out his appendix, tonsils, treated him for all of his childhood diseases, and set his broken wrist. He had come to the clinic the last time four years ago to get his free missionary physical. Dr. Jensen's name had been a household word as long as he could remember, a man his parents respected, loved, and trusted. His only son had been drowned on a family water-skiing trip to Bear Lake.

Steve knew that the feeling wouldn't come. He had the memories, the words, images in his mind, but he could not bring back the emotion. His body felt heavy and dull, like soft metal. The things he had done in Vietnam had destroyed his capacity to feel. For nearly a month now, since his return home to Provo, he had wanted to touch things, lay his face against them, for it was as if he were more than deaf, dumb, and blind. He needed to use every square inch of his burning skin to feel, make his whole body a receiver tuned to emotion. He wanted to put his arms around people on the street he didn't even know, embrace trees, press against old buildings; he was afraid he was going insane. God and Jesus had become only pictures. He had been drafted two days after he got back from his mission.

Steve had walked late at night to look at the houses of the girls he had gone with. Most of the girls were married now, had children. He looked at the places in front of their houses where he had parked with the girls. He had gone to their parties, been invited to dinners by their mothers. He kissed the girls good-night on their porches. He knew which windows were the girls' bedrooms. But standing in the darkness looking at the houses, his arms folded tight across his chest, he had felt nothing. It was as if he had never known the girls, and had no rich memories he could use of the laughter and warmth.

His mother mentioned the names of his old girl friends who were still single, but he did not phone them. His brothers had come home to see him. It was like talking to them under water or through thick glass. He wanted to wear gloves when he was around people. He was afraid that some little boy might ask him how many people he had killed.

Steve climbed the four steps from the clinic foyer to the waiting room. The big framed picture of Custer's last stand still hung on the wall above the radiator. The last man on his feet, Custer stood at the center of his dead and wounded men, a kneeling sergeant holding up the American flag on Custer's right side. Custer, a

56

pistol in each hand, his long yellow hair blowing in the breeze, shot at two mounted war chiefs charging him from opposite directions with raised lances. Braves jumped from their horses to kill the wounded soldiers. Dozens of braves lay dead or wounded. Steve had learned all the faces as a boy.

Mrs. Anderson sat at the reception desk talking to a man sitting on the green leather sofa. The man's right leg had been cut off just below the knee; a pair of crutches leaned against the wall behind him. The man's garments showed through his short-sleeved white shirt. The aquarium, yellow with afternoon light, stood before the large window. Mrs. Anderson turned. "Well, *Steve,* how nice to see you home again safe and sound. I noticed that one of the girls had made an appointment for you. I've talked to your mother in church about you. You've been home two or three weeks now haven't you?"

Steve took a *Life* from the magazine rack. "Yes."

"Mr. Simmons, you may not know Steve. He just got back from Vietnam. Before that he was on a mission for the Church in California, so he's been gone over four years altogether." The phone rang.

"Is that right, son? Well, welcome home." Mr. Simmons leaned forward to shake his hand. "Always glad to see you boys get home from Vietnam in one piece. I was in the first war myself."

Steve sat down on the black leather chair next to the aquarium, but he didn't open the *Life.* Mrs. Anderson pushed one of the buttons and put the phone back in the cradle. "Steve and my boy Richard were baptized and confirmed on the same days. I have a picture of them standing together in their white clothes. They were so sweet. They grew up together.

57

Richard is married and in dental school." She looked over at Steve. "How does it feel to be back home, Steve? Your parents certainly are grateful to have you back all safe and sound, aren't they."

"Yes." Richard hadn't gone on a mission or been in the army.

"But we haven't seen you out to church. I asked the bishop if he had seen you."

"I haven't made it yet."

"Oh."

The bishop had come by the house to welcome him home, and the president of the elders quorum had phoned twice to invite him to play on the ward softball team. Behind Mrs. Anderson on top of the first filing cabinet was a display rack of the Book of Mormon and three tracts, "Joseph Smith Tells His Own Story," "The Plan of Salvation," and "A Practical Gospel." Dr. Jensen had been a bishop for ten years, and now he was in the Provo Stake Presidency. He prayed before every operation he performed, and his patients often asked him to bless them.

Steve's body was very heavy. He never thought any more about having the priesthood. He had always liked the idea of God the Father and Jesus Christ. Things slipped in and out of focus. He was afraid he would forget how to tie his shoes or to button his shirt. He had lettered in tennis and basketball at Provo High.

"Have you found a job yet, Steve?"

"No." He opened the magazine.

"What are you doing with all of your spare time before school starts at B.Y.U.?"

"I don't know. I like to listen to music." He had bought over a hundred dollars worth of new records. He lay in the dark in his room and tried to keep his burning body full of soft sound. He wanted to fade into the darkness and the sound. He had always had a sense of order.

"Well, you boys who have been in Vietnam deserve to rest a week or two before you get back into harness. I guess you were able to do a lot of missionary work with your army friends while you were in Vietnam and preach the gospel, weren't you Steve? I understand that some returned missionaries make more converts in the army than they do on their missions because they're such good examples."

"I suppose that some of them do." He had thought that he could never lose what he had felt the two years he was on his mission in southern California. Elder Decker had been killed outside of Bien Hoa in an ambush. They knelt to pray together three and four times a day by the bunk beds, bore their testimonies to each other before they went out each morning tracting, had a scripture memorization contest going. They testified daily to the truthfulness of the gospel, Jesus Christ, the atonement, redemption; they blessed the sick, performed marriages; and, dressed in white, they baptized, felt that they were walking on air half the time because they had so many good investigators. Eight months after his release Elder Decker was in Vietnam.

They washed their garments themselves in the sink, always joking about what the girls back home would say. He had to stop himself from thinking about Elder Decker, control his mind so that he wouldn't turn completely to soft metal. His mother had sent him the *Church News* and the *Improvement Era*, but after the first month in Vietnam he couldn't read them anymore. His battalion had gone in twice to rescue ambushed outfits. Both times it was the same. He had heard about Elder Decker through another returned missionary he met in Saigon.

The phone rang again. Steve turned the pages of the *Life* magazine. He had made his appointment for Wednesday afternoon because he didn't want to be in the waiting room with a lot of other patients. Dr. Monson and Dr. Harris had Wednesday off. He didn't like people talking. One day when he had an appointment for a pre-school physical, a man had screamed from one of the rooms down the hall, "Oh, Jesus Christ! Oh, Jesus Christ! Oh, Jesus Christ!" The screaming came through the closed hall door, and for those seconds afterward no one in the waiting room moved or talked, the only other sound the bubbling from the oxygenator in the aquarium.

Mrs. Anderson put the phone back in the cradle.

Twice he had seen blood trails that started out in the parking lot, led up the steps, across the tile floor, to vanish down the hall. One of the girls came out with a damp cloth to wipe up the blood. All three doctors had gone rushing out one afternoon when he sat with his mother waiting. The sound of sirens vibrated through the big window in front of the aquarium, but his mother wouldn't let him go outside. Later, when they walked up University Avenue, he saw where the accident had been, although the cars had been towed off by then. The intersection was sprinkled with headlight glass, a big stain of radiator fluid on the black asphalt, as if a large animal had been killed there. He had read that over fifty thousand Americans were killed every year in automobile accidents and millions of others injured.

"Steve, this isn't serious is it?"

60

He looked up from the magazine. Mrs. Anderson had taken his manila folder from one of the fireproof filing cabinets and held it open on her desk. "It's a skin problem. I ran out of salve the army gave me, and I need a prescription." He wanted to ask Mrs. Anderson for his folder. What had Dr. Jensen said about him since he was born? The eight fireproof filing cabinets with locks were full of medical histories in manila folders, all the things that Dr. Jensen and the other doctors knew about their patients and had forgotten they knew—diseases, accidents, operations, treatments, and prescriptions. Everybody in the stake liked to hear Dr. Jensen's sermons. He always spoke about Jesus Christ. He had a strong testimony. After his son's death at Bear Lake, he had sold his boat.

"Is it something you contracted while you were in Vietnam, Steve?"

"Yes."

"Those jungles must be terrible places to have to fight in, and I understand that you were right out fighting the whole year you were there. My husband always says that as long as he had to fight, he was glad it was in France and Germany. He was in the war."

"I fought in France in the first war." Mr. Simmons leaned forward on the green leather sofa. "It's been fifty years and I still haven't forgotten some of the things that happened over there. I don't know what I would have done all these years without the Church."

A large silver safety pin held the empty pant leg to the side of his hip.

"But it's so terrible when you think about all those boys still in hospitals." Mrs. Anderson closed the manila folder. "My sister's neighbor's boy was in Korea, and he's still in a mental ward in a veterans hospital at Denver. He was such a nice boy. Dr. Jensen was in the Pacific all during the war, Steve, and he has other skin patients. You're lucky to have a doctor with experience. Dr. Jensen is a wonderful man."

"Yes."

"Richard will have to go in the army after dental school, but he'll be a captain."

Steve said nothing; a woman came in to pay a bill.

The breast markings on Mr. Simmon's garments showed through his white shirt. Steve looked down at the big *Life* pictures. He found himself checking white shirts to see who wore garments. He had liked receiving the Melchizedek priesthood, going through the temple and wearing garments; he felt clean and safe. He had always believed there were things he could never do. But now everything seemed the same; he had lost his sense of opposites.

He knew that members mistook his T-shirt for garments. His mother washed his boxers and T-shirts, folded them, and put them in his drawer by his white garments, some of which he had worn on his mission. Neither she nor his father said anything. He had turned his father down on three fishing trips to Strawberry. He didn't want to be alone in the boat with his father all day.

Reaching down, Steve rubbed the inside of his ankle. At times his whole body burned faintly. The army doctor had told him that some men lost all control and lay in bed scratching themselves until they had deep infected sores. He had always liked the shower after he had played basketball or tennis. His body had always been light and clean. He knew that he had begun to stare at things.

"All right, Mr. Simmons, Dr. Jensen will see you

now." Steve looked up from the *Life* again. "Well, hello, Steve, how are you? It's nice to see you home again. Several people have mentioned you were back."

Mrs. Bryce stood by the open hallway door in her white nurse's cap and uniform. She stepped into the waiting room to let Mr. Simmons swing through the door on his crutches. Steve stood up. "Thank you."

"You've been away four years haven't you, what with your mission and then the army?"

"I was discharged early."

"Well, now that you have that all behind you, you can start school again at B.Y.U. and get married like all of the rest of the boys. I'll bet you wrote to half a dozen girls while you were gone." He sat back down on the black leather chair.

Mrs. Anderson handed Mrs. Bryce his manila folder with a pink charge slip clipped to it. "I don't think that Dr. Jensen will be very long, Steve. Mr. Simmons is just in for a check-up and a change on his prescription." Turning, she closed the hall door behind her.

"Richard and his wife are expecting a baby, Steve. Did your mother tell you?"

"Yes."

A woman came into the clinic with a little girl who needed a shot, and Mrs. Anderson sent them back to the lab. The front cover of the old *Improvement Era* in the magazine rack was a picture of Joseph Smith's first vision. God the Father stood in bright light, his hand extended toward Jesus. The large white letters said, "This is my Beloved Son. Hear him." He didn't feel like he deserved anything now.

"Rita is a lovely girl and comes from a nice family. Her father is a doctor. Of course Richard and Rita plan to go on a mission together someday after they get their family raised. Richard thinks that maybe the Church will send them down to fix teeth for the Navajos. They had a beautiful reception." Mrs. Anderson got a plastic accordion packet of pictures from her purse in the desk drawer. "These are Richard's wedding pictures, Steve." She stood up, walked over to Steve, pulled a chair up to his, and explained every picture.

"We're all so proud of him." She stood up. "He wants to serve his tour of duty in Europe or Japan." She walked back to her desk and sat down. "What are you going to major in, Steve?"

"I don't know. I'm not certain any more that I want to go to college."

"Oh, but of course you want to go to college, Steve. Your mother and father would be very very disappointed if you didn't earn at least your bachelor's degree. Your three brothers all graduated after their missions didn't they?"

"Yes."

"Why, what would you do if you didn't go on to finish college?"

"I don't know."

"I thought that you wanted to go to law school at one time."

"I did."

"That's a fine profession. Your family would be proud of you." Mrs. Anderson turned to answer the phone.

The big window silhouetted the aquarium. The metallic fish flickered through the sunlit yellow water. The glass was smudged. As a little boy he had always pressed against the salty glass with his palms, nose, and lips. Fish floated in the rivers after artillery or bombs. He had followed blood trails and found monkeys and small jungle deer, not men. One platoon had found a tiger curled in the grass as if asleep, dead from concussion.

The hall door opened and Mr. Simmons swung through on his crutches, Mrs. Bryce behind him. "We'll see you next week again, Mr. Simmons." She handed Mrs. Anderson the pink charge slip.

"Thank you very much." He held his white prescription in his hand.

"Come in, Steve. Dr. Jensen will see you now."

"Lots of luck, son, now that you're back home."

Steve turned as he walked through the doorway. "Thank you."

Mrs. Bryce closed the door and followed him down the hall. "In here as usual, Steve. Just sit down. Dr. Jensen will be with you in a minute. He's in the lab." Mrs. Bryce closed the door behind her.

Steve rubbed under his belt, then raised his arms to the armrests. He had sat in the brown leather chair last when he had his missionary physical. He had been in perfect health, and he had felt very clean. Dr. Jensen gave all new missionaries from Provo Stake their physicals free. Since his son's death he paid to keep a missionary in the field. Steve looked up at the two yellowish windows. He had his missionary slides, and his mother had saved all of his missionary letters.

He lay on his bed at night to see his slides over and over, set the projector on automatic, stacked his hi-fi with records, and so saw on his wall all the lost images again, sound and images blurred, members, converts, companions in color. He had over a dozen slides with Elder Decker on them; he was always smiling. In his letters to his mother and father he had told what a great missionary Elder Decker was. Half of Elder Decker's squad had been killed with him in the ambush.

Steve had gone through his book of remembrance, the family photo albums, and all of his old high school yearbooks looking for himself. He looked at the pictures of the girls he had gone with. He got his little wooden box of Boy Scout badges out and his merit badge sash; in his book of remembrance he read his birth, blessing, and baptismal certificates and his priesthood ordination certificates. He had thought that when he saw his mother and father at the Salt Lake Airport his heart would leap just as it had when he returned from his mission, his body alive with memory, pride, gratitude, and love, but that had not happened. And it had not happened either when they drove around the point of the mountain and down into Utah Valley, the lights of Provo bright before them.

He went alone to places he had felt emotion—the Provo High gym, tennis courts, and locker room, the ward chapel, every room in the house, familiar streets under familiar trees, places he used to park with his dates, but he felt nothing. Two weeks ago on one of his long night drives, he swam out to the middle of Deer Creek Reservoir, hung naked there in the hundred-foot-deep water staring up at the moon and stars, his whole body cool, which he knew he could keep cool forever if he wanted.

Steve rubbed the right side of his groin. Dr. Jensen's license, medical school diploma, residency certificate in general surgery, and his army medical certificate hung on the wall over the examining table. The chrome, glass, and white enamel surfaces in the room gleamed in the diffused yellowish light. An open medical journal lay face down on the glass-topped desk by the pile of manila folders. The glass reflected Dr. Jensen's gold-framed family pictures. He had two pictures of his son. Worn copies of the *Articles of Faith, Jesus the Christ,* and the standard works stood in the row of books pushed against the wall. The pad of white prescription blanks lay next to the pen holder. Down the hall a phone rang.

"Well, hello, Steve. It's good to see you again." Dr. Jensen came in wiping his hands on a towel, his white jacket buttoned. He stepped on the foot pedal, dropped the towel into the large chrome container. He shook Steve's hand, his hand cool. "Well, you made it back I see."

"Yes."

"I think that your mother has counted every hour you were in Vietnam and said a thousand prayers. I guess you'll be finding a job and going to school at B.Y.U. this fall, and meeting a girl. The sooner you returned missionaries and servicemen get married, the better. You're going into law aren't you?"

"I don't know."

"Oh, I thought that was all decided."

"I don't know any more."

"Well, there are lots of good jobs if you're willing to work hard enough. Find something you like and work hard at it. Too many people go through life never knowing what they want."

Dr. Jensen looked down at his opened manila folder, adjusted his bifocals. "You've got some kind of skin problem, Steve? Something you brought back from Vietnam with you I suppose?"

"Yes. It's on my army medical records, but I don't want to have to go to Salt Lake to the V.A. Hospital every time I need some salve."

"Where does it bother you the most? Between your toes, around your genitals, under your arms, where you sweat? It burns doesn't it?"

"Yes."

"Go behind the screen and undress. You can roll your garments down to your waist."

Steve stripped down tc his shorts and walked back out, the tile cool on his feet. Dr. Jensen glanced at him, then pulled the long-necked lamp over to the white metal chair. "Sit down here." The cool metal chilled Steve. Pushing the lamp in so close that Steve felt the heat from the bulb, Dr. Jensen examined along his hair line, behind his ears, had him stand up and hold out each arm, told him to drop his shorts. "Any chance of venereal disease, Steve?"

"No."

"Okay, good. Put your shorts back on and sit on the table." Dr. Jensen examined between his toes, then straightened up. "It looks like some kind of fungus to me. I can tell you right now that your scratching it hasn't helped any. I can send you to the hospital for some tests if you want or to a skin specialist, but I suppose that the army has already done that."

"Yes. I just want a salve to stop the burning until the weather cools off. They said it would be better when the weather got cooler." He wanted to tell Dr. Jensen how his body was like soft metal that he couldn't feel.

Dr. Jensen sat down at his desk and started to write out the prescription. "It will be better in cooler weather. And it will die down for six months or a year, then flare up again. Summer is the worst because you sweat. I can name you a dozen men here in Provo who still have it from the last war. I have had this prescription made up that helps, but it's one of those things you're going to have to learn to live with. One way or another we all have something."

"I know."

"I doubt that you do, but you may in ten or fifteen years. You can get dressed." Dr. Jensen didn't raise his head.

When Steve came out from behind the screen, Dr. Jensen told him to sit down. Dr. Jensen leaned back in his chair, his head silhouetted against the pale yellow window. "It didn't bother you did it when I asked if there was any chance of a venereal disease?"

"No."

"It would have before you went to Vietnam."

"I guess."

"Two years ago you'd have been insulted that I could even think that of you. Now you don't wear your garments and you haven't been to church since you got back."

"My mother and father have been talking to you."

"No, they haven't, but other people have. You've been home nearly a month now. A lot of people love you, Steve. Everybody's always thought of you as a fine young person."

"They shouldn't."

"Why not?"

"You couldn't understand." Dr. Jensen turned to answer the phone. Steve looked a little to the right of his face. The chrome and glass in the room reflected distorted images. He had needed his own private movie cameraman with him every minute. He could show the movies to all of his neighbors, friends, and relatives. He could sit in his bedroom and watch himself over and over again daily, until perhaps he, too, knew what he had done. But the movies would have to be in black and white, silent, only images. He knew that his father had asked some of his old high school friends to call him to play tennis, but he always said no. Dr. Jensen had a fine spray of dry blood on the left sleeve of his white jacket.

Dr. Jensen put the receiver back in the cradle. "I might understand, Steve. I was in the Pacific for three years in the last war."

"You didn't fight."

"No, I operated. We worked in teams; we operated ten and twelve hours straight when the fighting was heavy. After a week or two of that, you've cut off and cut out everything a man can lose and still live."

"It isn't the same."

"No, it isn't entirely the same I guess. You lost a former missionary companion in Vietnam didn't you? Your mother did tell me that one day when she was in."

"I didn't tell her."

"She saw his obituary in one of the Salt Lake papers. She didn't want to tell you if you didn't know."

"They cut off his head."

"That's bad."

"We did things like that to them."

"I suppose you did." Dr. Jensen paused. "One winter back in the 1850s my grandfather was one of the Provo settlers who chased about twenty-five Ute Indians out on the Utah Lake ice and killed them in a running fight. A doctor took a sled out, cut all of their heads off, treated them, and then sent them East for a medical museum skull collection."

"Is that supposed to help me?"

"You need to know that that kind of thing happens fairly often."

"Does it?"

"You had a missionary companion wounded, too, didn't you?"

"He wasn't my companion. We were in the same district."

"What happened to him?"

"He stepped on a mine and it blew off both his legs."

"How did he take it?"

"He tried to commit suicide in the hospital in Japan."

Steve rubbed the side of his neck.

"You should try not to do that, Steve." Dr. Jensen laid both of his hands, palms up, on the glass-topped desk. Heavy shadows showed through the yellowish opaque windows. When Elder Decker was made zone leader, transferred, they tried just to shake hands, but it wasn't enough, and they hugged each other. Steve had to keep fighting the image of the headless body in the sealed casket going back to Logan. Elder Decker had lettered in basketball and been a National Merit finalist. Steve couldn't let the casket get too big. A body could explode, the flesh and bones marring the trees, brush, and earth.

"I can name you men in Provo who saw and did worse things in the last war and in Korea, but they came home, got married, raised families, stayed active in the Church, honored their priesthood. Some of them even went on missions after they got back."

"They fought in a better war than I did."

"They killed other men, Steve. Do you plan to end up in a V.A. psycho ward?" The glass-topped desk

71

mirrored the backs of Dr. Jensen's hands. His gold wedding band glinted. "You should come out to the Utah Valley Hospital with me this afternoon, Steve."

"Why?"

"I've got a little four-year-old boy in the hospital with third-degree burns all over his head, face, and shoulders. His mother knocked a pan of boiling water off of the stove on top of him. And you might want to talk to Dr. Franceman. He delivered a blind baby boy Thursday. The mother is thirty-five and has four children. Her husband infected her with gonorrhea. You remember Kelly Tolman; he played basketball for B.Y.U. about six years ago. He's in intensive care with a fractured skull and two broken legs. He apparently fell asleep driving back from Salt Lake Wednesday night, sideswiped a semi-truck, and killed his wife. Some car accidents can even be worse than a hand grenade or a mortar shell."

Dr. Jensen looked at the gold-framed pictures. His son's name was David.

"You didn't start to drink or go on drugs, and you didn't sleep with any Vietnamese whores."

"No, I just killed people."

"Don't ever become a surgeon."

"They save lives."

"No, they just prolong them, sometimes." Dr. Jensen looked down at his open hands. "You saw old Ralph Simmons on his crutches." Dr. Jensen nodded toward the pile of manila folders. "He's got diabetes and I had to amputate his leg below the knee four months ago, but I didn't go high enough. Now I've got to take as much of his leg as I can."

Dr. Jensen slowly closed his hands. "You can't love or forgive yourself enough, Steve, and nobody else

72

can either, although they can help. All of us need somebody like Jesus Christ for that. At least it's the only answer I've found that makes any sense."

Dr. Jensen sat looking at his closed hands, and then the phone rang. "I'll be there in ten minutes," he said, and hung up.

Dr. Jensen stood up, unbuttoned his white jacket, hung it on the chrome coat tree, and put on his suit coat. He closed Steve's manila folder and set it on the pile. "Get this prescription filled at City Drug. They make it for some other patients of mine. You might as well get used to that burning during this hot weather, but you'll be a lot better off if you don't scratch it." The neckline of Dr. Jensen's garments showed through his white shirt. He wrote on the pink charge slip. "There's no charge, Steve. Use the money for school next month."

"I have money."

"I know that. Try to accept things people want to give you. And here's some more advice. Start going to church. You're not better or worse than most of us. And get married. You need to hold a wife in your arms for about six weeks to thaw you out."

Steve walked down the hall ahead of Dr. Jensen. "Say hello to your mom and dad for me." He turned to Mrs. Anderson at the desk and gave her the pink slip. "There's no charge on Steve."

"Yes, Doctor Jensen."

"Goodbye, Steve. I'm glad you're home." He shook Steve's hand. "I'll be at the hospital, Mrs. Anderson." Carrying his black bag, he walked across the waiting room and down the foyer steps.

"Dr. Jensen is a wonderful man. We need more in the world like him. There isn't anything he wouldn't do for the Church."

"No, I guess there isn't."

"You weren't wounded or anything were you, Steve? I suppose I would have heard if you had been."

"No, I wasn't wounded."

"I prayed night and morning on my knees that Richard wouldn't be drafted and have to go to Vietnam. I know that was selfish of me, but I couldn't help it, Steve. I cried every time I saw a picture in the *Herald* of one of the boys who had been killed. I guess we can't even guess how terrible it was for you boys. If my Richard didn't go, somebody else's boy had to. I suppose that I was very selfish. I hope the Lord will forgive me for that."

He turned. Silhouetted by the light from the window, the goldfish flashed against the side of the aquarium, the water yellow with sunlight. The oxygenator made a noise. "Mothers should say that kind of prayer, I guess."

Mrs. Bryce came down the hall. "Well, Steve, I suppose that the next time we see you it will be for a blood test for getting married."

He folded the prescription Dr. Jensen had given him and put it in his shirt pocket. "Maybe."

"Of course it will be. You boys don't stay single long, and you'll make some girl a fine husband. Don't waste any of those wonderful years. It's good to see you back, Steve." Mrs. Bryce turned and walked back down the hall without closing the door. There were no more patients waiting.

"Steve," Mrs. Anderson said, "if I hear of any part-time jobs for school, I'll let you know."

"Thank you." He walked across the waiting room but stopped by the picture of Custer's last stand. Custer shot at the two mounted charging war chiefs with his over-sized silver pearl-handled pistols. He had a blood-stained bandage tied around his forehead, one arrow sticking in his right leg, another arrow in his left hip. Eleven Indians lay dead in front of Custer. Steve turned away from the picture. Mrs. Anderson sat looking across her desk at the aquarium. "Tell Richard hello for me when you write him next time, Mrs. Anderson," he said.

"Oh, thank you, Steve, I will." She reached to pick up the ringing telephone.

Steve walked down the steps and pushed open the door. Outside, he put on his sunglasses and checked to see that he had the prescription in his shirt pocket. He walked along Second South and turned up University Avenue toward the City Drug. By the time he got to the City and County Building, he felt the burning, as if someone were touching him with a sponge dipped in a weak acid solution. He slowly curled his fingers.

Swinging her shoulder purse by the strap, a girl wearing sandals walked just ahead of him. Her long dark hair fell to her waist. Steve crossed Center Street and stood by the door of the City Drug. He took off his sunglasses. She stopped to look in Allen's window. She swung her purse gently across her legs, and her shining dark hair fell down over her bare arm. Steve stood there for a moment after she walked into Allen's, and then he turned and pushed open the heavy glass door.

ELDER THATCHER

All through the sacrament service, David still watched to see if Todd Campbell came in. David's mother and father sat on one side of him, Bishop Fielding and the stake president on the other. David took out his handkerchief again and dried his palms. He held his triple combination and Bible on his knee. He felt stiff in his new clothes.

Twenty people had been at dinner; his mother had invited the whole family, and Jane. Just before it was time to leave to come to church, he'd gone outside to be alone for a minute. He was standing at the end of the driveway when Todd Campbell, who had worked for his father two years at the station, drove by, stopped, backed up, and swung into the curb. He stuck his head out the window.

"It's your welcome home today isn't it, Dave?"

"Yes, at four."

"Well, try not to tell them any more lies than you have to."

"What do you mean?"

"You'll know when you stand up at that pulpit.

You returned missionaries are all the same."

"What?"

"Maybe I'll come just to hear what you say."

Just then David's family had started coming out of the house, and Todd drove off. "Was that Todd Campbell driving that car?" his mother asked.

"Yes."

"Nobody knows what's happened to that boy. He's broken his family's heart since his mission though, I know that. He should have gotten married."

David looked down the street. Todd had dropped out of the Church within six months after he got home from his mission. He lived in their ward.

As they drove to sacrament meeting, theirs the first of the five cars with the family, David had watched the familiar houses. He remembered something that Elder Cummings, his last junior companion, had said: "Just for kicks you ought to try tracting Provo when you get home, Elder Thatcher. But just for kicks."

David looked at the pulpit. Two years ago at his farewell he had stood there and said, "I know that the gospel of Jesus Christ is true, that the Book of Mormon is true, that God lives, that Jesus is the Christ, and that Joseph Smith was and is a prophet of God." Gripping the sides of the pulpit, his hands sweaty, he had felt the whole ward needed him to say that. He saw what they wanted him to say to confirm their idea of what a newly ordained nineteen-year-old elder should be. When he sat down again between his parents, his mother gripped his hand, wiped the tears from her eyes with her handkerchief. His father reached over to grip his knee. Until that afternoon he had never heard his father or mother bear their testimonies.

After the meeting, relatives, friends, and ward

members said, "David, you'll be a wonderful missionary for the Lord. You have a wonderful testimony now, but think what it will be when you get back. We're all proud of you." They shook his hand, hugged him, slipped five- and ten-dollar bills into his jacket pocket. He hadn't read the Book of Mormon; he'd skipped priesthood about a third of the time; he didn't say his personal prayers; and he and Jane had made out until the day Bishop Fielding called him in his office to ask him if he wanted to go on a mission.

David looked past the pulpit down at the ward, the rows of faces, everybody smiling, the whole ward happy for him, ready to hear his talk. The folded two-page typed outline was in his inside pocket. He'd started going back through his missionary journal to mark things a month ago and had finished the talk last night. He had wanted to give a great talk, make it his gift to the whole ward for all of the things they had done for him, and let it be the official end of his mission.

He had been home ten days. He worked at his father's station again, was registered for fall semester at B.Y.U., dated Jane, had bought another VW, and he had been so happy that he'd felt dizzy, almost stunned, full of love and gratitude, his life as good as it could ever be, all the required changes made. He still sometimes thought in German, forgot and used German words, which made people smile. At first he had been lost without a companion and the daily routine of missionary work, but in the last two or three days there had been moments when he had to think about his mission to remember it, as if it were possible to forget the whole two years.

At night his first days home, after his date with

Jane, he rode his bicycle up and down the familiar Provo streets under the trees. At first he had thought that everything and everyone in Provo had changed, but then he realized that it was himself, and that change was proof of what had happened to him on his mission, how he was new, which he couldn't have understood in Germany.

President Maxwell had said, "Don't be surprised when you get home, Elder Thatcher."

"What do you mean?"

"It's something nobody can explain to you. It's a discovery a good missionary makes. Just be careful."

The talk he had prepared was full of experiences, how he had come to love the Book of Mormon, how his converts, Brother and Sister Schindler, Brother Schwartz, and Brother Binderwald, had changed their lives when they became members, how happy they became. He had blessed the sick, prayed, fasted, preached, borne testimony of Jesus Christ, experienced the Holy Ghost, so he knew that spiritual experience was something you felt in your whole body, which you couldn't deny because you had felt it and you knew that you had. It had made him feel lifted up, purified, aware of so much possibility that it scared him. He'd only heard returned missionaries tell the good things about their missions. He wanted to make everybody happy.

The deacons, standing in front of the sacrament table, took the water; the three priests unfolded the white linen tablecloth to spread it over the trays. The ward stirred a little, members coughing, stretching. The family all sat together on three middle rows. His mother had written or phoned everybody. His Uncle Ralph hadn't come; he'd gone on a mission to France but had quit the Church years ago, before David was even born.

He looked down at Elders Spencer, Grey, and Norton, who all sat on the same row with their girls. They had all been released from the mission before he was. They grinned. They had already given their talks; now they wanted to hear what he would say about the Central German Mission. Elder Norton had brought a blonde named Ramona. "Preach repentance unto these sinners, Elder Thatcher," he had said out in the foyer, laughed, put his arm around Ramona's shoulders, hugged her so that her right foot raised off the floor. All the elders looked different than he had remembered them. They looked relieved, satisfied, happy in a different way, wore new clothes. None had brought their scriptures with them. The only way to tell that some elders had been on missions was that you could see the garments under their shirts.

He looked down at his hands. He'd been able, finally, on his mission to forget about his body, not even be aware of it, as if it had become air or light, or some special kind of rare metal. He looked down at Jane, who sat next to his Grandmother Arnold. They'd dated every night the last week. Already they were talking about getting married; there wasn't anything else to do. They went to shows, watched TV, played tennis, went for long drives, and he ate at her house at least once a day. Praying seemed strange without a companion; he didn't need to bear testimony a dozen times a day now.

At least fifteen people had said just yesterday and today, "David, we expect a wonderful testimony from you in sacrament meeting. We heard you had a marvelous mission. You must have had a lot of faith-

81

promoting experiences."

"Scott gave a wonderful talk at his welcome home, son," his mother had said.

Scott sat on the left side of the chapel with his parents and a girl named Cindy that David didn't know. Ron sat at the back with Marsha, who had waited for him. Dan would get home from Mexico in two weeks.

For him, Ron, Dan, and Scott, all best friends, to be made elders at nineteen and go on missions was to be clean and do what their parents and everybody else had wanted them to do all of their lives. In the weeks before their missions, when they saw each other, they said, "Hey, elder," laughed, shook hands. They felt splendid, had confessed all of their sins to their bishops, thought that everybody else was splendid too, at nineteen their lives already practical, already changed. They didn't need to ski anymore, own cars, buy new clothes every week, watch TV, have or be with girls.

They became fierce in their desire to repay all their parents' love by being perfect, which meant to do and believe all those things they had been taught in Primary, Junior Sunday School, Boy Scouts, priesthood, and seminary. They had to be examples for their little brothers. Their mothers took them out to the University Mall and Z.C.M.I. to buy all new clothes because they didn't want them to wear anything old on their missions. Scott's mother had gone with him to buy his garments.

Resting his Bible and triple combination on his knee, David slipped his hand inside his jacket and took out his talk. He unfolded the two pages and read through the outline twice. He raised his head slowly, looked out at the ward. He hadn't put in anything about the first part of his mission, just the last year. He read through the outline again; he looked at all the back rows for Todd Campbell. He wasn't there. The back doors were still closed because of the sacrament. He slowly folded the talk and slipped it back into his pocket.

He'd even been homesick in the LTM, was still in Provo but already homesick, didn't want to leave his friends, Jane, all the other girls he knew, his family, their house, the Provo mountains, everything he knew and loved. Three times he saw his VW; the guy he'd sold it to didn't keep it waxed. Memorizing the scriptures and discussions in German, getting up at six, studying twelve hours a day, all the discipline—it was all too hard, harder than anything he'd ever done.

But going to Germany was even worse. The flight from Salt Lake to Frankfurt put him in another world. Everything was different—the food, houses, trees, clothes, buildings, even the smells, colors, and noises.

He was so scared he was almost sick. He didn't want to leave the mission home in Frankfurt, get on the train, go to Giessen to work with Elder Harris, his senior companion. He wanted to ask President Maxwell if he could be a file clerk, the gardner, the janitor, anything just so he didn't have to go out and tract.

The homesickness in Germany was worse even than at the LTM, became an ache in his whole body, as if his body could only be happy in Provo, his eyes suddenly filling with tears. He felt like a kid, but his love for home was the strongest emotion he had ever known, and he longed all day for it to be night so he could go to bed.

He was embarrassed all the time because he made

mistakes speaking German, because of the public baths, because he couldn't keep his clothes always clean, because there was only one hall toilet for three apartments on the floor where he and Elder Harris had a room. He didn't want the priesthood or to be an elder; he wanted to wear T-shirts and shorts again, not garments. He hated the self-discipline, studying German, studying scriptures.

The train had arrived in Giessen just before noon, and by two Elder Harris had him out tracting. "We're missionaries, Elder Thatcher," he said. "What did you think we would do this afternoon?"

Elder Harris made him take the second door, and he froze, was struck dumb. He stood waiting for Elder Harris to save him, but he didn't. The German woman laughed.

"You are American?" she asked in good English.

"*Ja.*" He had been able to say that.

"Thank you, no, I do not need your American God." She handed him the tract again, closed the door, but he still heard her laughter through the glass.

In spite of all the new buildings in the cities, Germany was old, the villages old, with medieval castles and battle towers silhouetted on the hills. And he sensed that the Germans feared something they would not, or could not, name. Germans tried hard to enjoy themselves, particularly the young Germans.

Brother Klempau of the Giessen Branch always covered his face with both hands during the sacrament, bowed his head almost to his knees. He worked in a German military hospital as a male nurse. Every day he gave drugs to kill the pain from wounds thirty years old. He nursed the blind, deaf, dumb, and insane; he knew all the sounds, smells, and visions of human misery. And before they had all died, he nursed armless, legless men who hung in baskets, lowered and raised them on pulleys, put diapers on men fifty years old. Brother Klempau had been one of the first converts after the war. When he bore his testimony he said, "Only faith in the Lord Jesus Christ can make life possible and give it meaning. Only a power outside of us can make us change. The gospel of Jesus Christ is very practical."

David dried his palms on his handkerchief again. The deacons had all taken their seats. His mother leaned over to whisper something to his father. David looked over at the priests sitting at the sacrament table.

Before he went to Germany he had never heard people tell personal stories of suffering, atrocities, starvation, death, stories of whole families, neighborhoods, and cities destroyed. He had not known that guilt, terror, and despair could last thirty years, stop life. All the countries in Europe were small and close together; people in the whole world had to change. He had never needed a Savior to pay for all the man-caused suffering, the evil, had never been scared that way. Without payment there could be no justice, and without justice, no meaning. It all became finally reasonable to him. There had to be someone capable of forgiving man.

But he hadn't wanted to have to live by testimony, do all the things that a testimony and having the priesthood would require him to do. He didn't want to study the scriptures, pray all the time, love, become humble, live by faith, seek the Holy Ghost in all he did, follow the Lord, have a new mind and a new heart, have that kind of understanding and power. He had never really thought what it meant to prepare the world for the coming of the Lord. But if he wanted to stay honest, he had no choice, because he knew that promises were being kept.

He had new feelings, but not chills, a lump in his throat, not crying. It began to feel good to study the scriptures; it made him happy. He began to love Elder Harris, felt that tense melting feeling in his chest. He could kneel down and pray, say things he'd never said before in prayers or needed to say. He felt like he was expanding inside his mind, in his whole body, his body feeling better than it ever had before, stronger and different. But it wasn't so much at first that he could affirm all of these feelings as that he couldn't deny them, which he couldn't, and he knew it.

It surprised him now that in ten days home he didn't feel things like he had in the mission field. His life was different, but he had thought he would always have those feelings and never have to change again. But now it was as if the feelings couldn't last, be kept in his memory; now he had to go further and turn the experience into ideas, define what had happened, know the meaning, and accept it, so that it would be his forever and let him do other things. He'd been so happy to be home that he hardly stopped to think how he felt. He didn't have a companion, didn't do missionary work every day all day, think only about that, have only those experiences and feelings. He watched TV, went to movies, played tennis, worked at the station, and dated Jane, his life comfortable. He didn't have to worry so much about being honest.

Bishop Fielding stood up and walked to the pulpit. Priests sat in the congregation with their girls; the priests liked to hear missionary welcome-home talks.

86

David knew that their parents would not want him to describe in detail how a priest got pressured into going on a mission. He had heard that a lot of returned missionaries became inactive.

When he'd asked his father about going on a mission, his father had said, "It's something I wouldn't want you to miss, son." His mother and everybody else had simply always assumed that he would go. He and his father never talked about priesthood.

It was as if all the love, kindness, all the good things everybody had done for him, the way they had respected and praised him, were meant only to force him into going on his mission, obligate him to do that. After he turned eighteen all he heard was, "When are you going on your mission, Dave? Had your interview yet? It will be a great experience for you, but a big change too to serve the Lord twenty-four hours a day." It was as if for them nothing else could have any meaning in his life and he could have no other desire. Elders like Smith, Watson, Nelson, and Williams never got over feeling they had been tricked.

The Biology Department at B.Y.U. did tests for blood and intestinal parasites on students who had served missions in Central and South America, the Philippines, and Asia, and found that one in three was infected. Dave had heard of one elder who had ten to twelve bowel movements a day because of amoebic dysentary, which no doctor had been able to cure.

Holding his Bible and triple combination on his knee with his left hand, David took out his talk again and unfolded it on his other knee. It was all about the last part of his mission, the great part. He had left out the first eight months, but he hadn't told any lies. He had just tried to write the best talk he could. He slowly folded the talk and slipped it back into his jacket pocket.

Bishop Fielding was making an announcement he had forgotten earlier.

David looked down at his scriptures, which he held with both hands now. The leather covers were all worn, pages loose. The gold edging was all gone; nearly every page was marked.

Elder Harris had made him study. At six every morning when Elder Harris had said in German, "Time to hit it, Elder Thatcher," he had crawled down under the blankets, wanted only to stay deep in the warmth and darkness, smother if necessary, just not have to get up to go tracting, be embarrassed all day. He wanted people to call him by his first name, say David or Dave, not call him elder all the time and use only his last name. He said his first name to himself just to hear it, liked to read it on his letters. The Germans couldn't pronounce the "th" sound in his last name.

He had hated Elder Harris for working so hard, enjoying missionary work, for only speaking German to him, for expecting so much from him, telling him about the power the Lord was willing to give him if he earned it. But he hated him most for his strong testimony and for having only eleven months left until he was released. Elder Harris had been one of those missionaries who come into the mission field already with a strong testimony. Some days he'd wanted to punch Elder Harris, just give him one good punch right in the mouth just to see what he would do.

"Time for prayer, Elder Thatcher." They kneeled to pray after they got up in the morning, kneeled again before they left for tracting, again after lunch, before and after every discussion with a contact, kneeled to pray a dozen times a day, ask for direction, humility, faith, the companionship of the Holy Ghost, the ability to love.

They had to seek the Holy Ghost in everything they did, depend on his guidance, deny their own bodies and minds, not depend only on themselves, as if suddenly they were no longer persons, didn't have bodies of their own. They had to have special power and strength to help spread the gospel of Christ over the whole earth, exercise their priesthood, act in the name of Jesus Christ, everything possible then. The gift of the Holy Ghost was heat, light, understanding, power, so that you were changed, felt and knew things you didn't before, which you couldn't deny. And you wanted to shout sometimes because it was so great, but you didn't.

Bishop Fielding cleared his throat. "Brothers and sisters, let me say again what a pleasure it is to have you all here at David's welcome home. I know that he has a fine message for us all, that we are all anxious to hear. But first his cousin Linda will sing a solo, and then we will hear just a word or two from his mother and father. Linda will announce her own number and the name of her accompanist."

Linda and his Aunt Grace walked down the left aisle. David counted his former Sunday School and priesthood teachers in the congregation. Everybody smiled, was happy, loved him. It was as if they already knew what he would say, already enjoying the series of faith-promoting stories that every missionary was supposed to bring back with him. As if the conversions, healings, testimonies were meant only to affirm what they believed, feed them, his love for them making him do that so they wouldn't be disappointed. No one had asked, in the ten days he'd been home, "Dave, what was your mission really like, can you tell me?" His mother planned to invite the whole ward over to the house for punch and cookies after the meeting. A dozen people in Sunday School had told him how nice he looked in his new clothes. His mother had bought him ten new pair of garments Wednesday, had put them in his drawer and taken his old garments.

The rear doors to the chapel opened; two young couples he didn't know came in. David felt his heart race a little. The doors closed; Todd Campbell hadn't come in.

Listening to Linda sing, David went up and down the rows to find the ward members who really had strong testimonies of the gospel—Sister Clark, Sister Nielsen, Brother and Sister Miller, the Heals and their family. He'd never thought about tracting the ward until Elder Cummings mentioned it three weeks ago in Frankfurt. Elder Cummings had said that every missionary should spend the last two months of his mission tracting his own ward. The gospel changed the whole lives of people who were about to get a divorce, were alcoholics, were on drugs, who wanted to commit suicide, had nothing to live for. The gospel made Brother and Sister Schindler, Brother Schwartz, and Brother Binderwald different people, changed their whole lives and how they acted.

David looked over at his father and mother. He'd thought that his mission would start his parents having kneeling family prayer. "Son, it's something your mother and I just don't do," his father had said Wednesday at the station when he asked him about it. "We pretty well take care of that when we bless the food. You'll have your own family soon, so you'll have your chance there."

David listened to Linda's solo. He'd heard about elders who, after a week or two home, wanted to go back on another mission because they couldn't stand being home. He looked down at Scott sitting between his mother and his girl. Of all of his friends in the mission field, Scott had written the most enthusiastic letters. He needed to have heard Scott's welcome-home talk. Before the meeting, when he was standing in the foyer greeting people with his parents, the stake president had put his hand on his shoulder and said, "We need a good talk tonight, Elder Thatcher."

David looked at his hands. He took out his handkerchief and wiped his palms. His Bible and triple combination were sweaty where he held them.

At first he had been afraid of getting old. Over two years on a mission, six in college at least, and maybe eight if he went beyond his master's degree, meant that he would be thirty before he finally got through. So he would never really be young and free again. He had hated the Church for forcing him to go on his mission. His mission would rob him of two of the happiest years of his life, the last of his real youth.

Out tracting with Elder Harris in Giessen, he kept thinking about his VW and all the good times he was missing in Provo. Mostly he thought about all the girls he would never go with during those two years in Germany; he could only write to girls and look at their pictures, say their names aloud to himself—Melissa, Sue, Stephanie, Melinda, Becky, Marnie, Jane.

He felt cheated, his body getting older every day, as if he were already dying at nineteen (he needed a

91

shower night and morning and all the clean clothes he wanted). And all the time he was supposed to be full of faith, be guided by the Holy Ghost, love the Lord, love the German people, love Elder Harris, magnify his priesthood. Spirituality and working twelve and fifteen hours a day weren't natural for a person just a year out of high school. Elder Stahlie, his first junior companion, had cried every day his first six weeks in Mannheim, before he finally started to get hold of himself.

David had not written home about his constant urge those first months to get away from Elder Harris somehow, rush back to the room, pack his stuff and leave without even phoning President Maxwell or telegraphing his parents. "Hello, Mom," he had planned to say when his mother answered the door, "I came home." He saw himself standing there on the porch after he rang the door bell (he would have to ring the door bell), a suitcase in each hand.

"Why, son?" she would say, her eyes suddenly filling with tears.

"I couldn't take it any longer, Mom. It wasn't what I expected. Nobody told me what it would really be like. It was too hard; I was embarrassed all the time. You couldn't even take a shower when you wanted."

Dan, Ron, and Scott would finish their missions, but he wouldn't if he went home. For the rest of his life, when he saw them or somebody asked him if he had been on a mission, he would feel guilty. People would never trust him again, and he would never be able to trust himself.

He had wanted to go home because of all the good things, all the people who loved him, his family, Jane, but that all trapped him on his mission, and his life wouldn't be the same if he went home. He couldn't imagine his life without the Church. But he had to be honest or everything lost meaning. It had surprised him how honest he wanted to be. It seemed terribly important to be honest or he lost a place to start his life. But he resented it that nobody had ever told him how hard a mission was, not even his father, or his uncles, who had all been on missions.

So he had decided that he could ask for a release and go home honest only if he did absolutely everything he was supposed to. Then he could stand up in testimony meeting and say, "I made an honest mistake. I found out that I didn't know the gospel was true, but I still want to go to church and live here in the ward with you. I don't need to be an elder or hold the priesthood. I love everybody, I love my family, I love the Church."

He listened to Linda sing the last verse. The slanting rays of the sun coming through the high narrow windows had turned the pulpit silver. A large chapel full of members was strange to him. The German Saints often met in small rented rooms where the older saints who had endured everything, always bore strong testimonies of the truthfulness of the practical gospel of Jesus Christ. Brother and Sister Schindler, Brother Schwartz, and Brother Binderwald, his converts, had all borne testimony. He liked small congregations better.

But it was incredible how members in some branches spread rumors, criticized, complained, were never satisfied with anything, as if the German Saints had a special talent for that; two or three members could destroy a whole branch.

Many Germans he tracted, especially the younger

93

ones, believed in nothing. He had never thought that a person's life could be so bad that it would teach him there was no resurrection, no eternal right and wrong, that change wasn't possible and you couldn't be perfect some day. He had suddenly found that he wanted the gospel to be true, and was scared at first that it might not be, the scriptures meaningless, fables, no special power or knowledge possible through the priesthood.

The young Germans they tracted tried to get them into arguments about America's waste of natural resources, Vietnam, Watergate, the American army's failure to join with the German Army and destroy the Russians at the end of World War II, and the stupidities of capitalism.

David watched his mother stand up and walk to the pulpit. She had her handkerchief in her hand. "It is a great thrill for us to welcome David home, brothers and sisters, and know that he has filled an honorable mission. We have thrilled to receive his letters as we have seen how he has grown in the gospel. We know that what he learned on his mission will be a great help to him all of his life."

His mother had saved twenty dollars a month for two years so that he could have new clothes when he got home. She had given his worn missionary shoes, socks, suits, shirts, and ties to the Deseret Industries. "Son," she had said, "you simply can't wear those things any longer. They may have been fine for the mission field, but you're home in Provo now."

He had his old room back; the furniture, wallpaper, even the bedding, were the same as when he left. His mother's wedding rings glistened; she held the sides of the pulpit. She believed that his whole mission had been wonderful. Tonight was a big part of her reward for sending him. He hadn't written lies in his letters, but he had never told how hard it was.

At first the hardest part was the public baths, dirty clothes, fear of losing his hair, growing fat on the German food, not feeling free or athletic any more, his body hidden from knee to neck by his garments. It was impossible to have to follow Elder Harris' example every day, get up at six, pray, study, tract for six hours, hold street meetings, cottage meetings, never be finished, and so be embarrassed all day.

It had been hard, knowing how much he was sacrificing every day he was away from Provo, and each day he longed for it to be night so that he could go to bed, cover his head with his pillow to shut out all sight and sound, imagine he was home, hope for dreams, find comfort that way. But the hardest part, finally, was knowing that he was supposed to love everybody, have faith, be like the Savior; he had to change the way he felt about things, and so create a discipline for his life, be happy and clean.

Elder Morton, his second junior companion, had four large framed pictures of his girl. He wrote her every night, talked only of her, and so paralyzed himself with memory and desire. Elder Brimley had a nervous breakdown, thought that he was a prophet, had to be sent home. Living only in the past or the future, some elders carried marked pocket calendars, and their first question was always, "How many months till you get released, Elder Thatcher?" Daily they tortured themselves with the memory of their happy lives at home. David had heard of elders who fought each other, came to conference with black eyes and cut lips.

But always there were those elders like Elders Farnsworth, Terry, Jorgenson, Heywood, Harris, who had a spirituality like a magnetic field around them that pulled you to them finally. It was in their faces, the alert, happy way they moved their bodies, and in their voices and words. They worked the hardest of all the elders, knew the scriptures, had a power and cleanness that he couldn't deny, loved. So he knew that the promises could be true; it was the only explanation. It was what he could have and be if he wanted; he could change, be different than he was, have all those promises kept, become as strong as they were, and know he held the priesthood.

Riding his bicycle out to the tracting area each morning, Elder Harris ahead of him as usual or riding along side to drill him on his vocabulary, David had needed either to vomit or to find a restroom.

At seventy-five doors a day average, leaving out diversion days, Sundays, and district, zone, and mission conferences, he had stood before at least fifty thousand German doors. But he had never gotten used to being laughed at, having a door slammed in his face, which was like being spit on. Twice he and his companion had been shouted at all the way down the stairs and cursed for being Americans. One German woman had run down the stairs after them holding a picture of her son burned alive in an American bombing raid on Nuremberg thirty years before and shouting, *"Seine Name war Hans! Seine Name war Hans! Seine Name war Hans!"*

When he and his companion came out of the German apartment houses, above them the German women leaned out their street windows on their arm pillows talking to each other about the crazy Americans, *die Mormonen*, laughing. He wondered now what would happen if the Church put all of the missionaries in Utah to tract only members and ask them if they accepted the promises of Jesus Christ.

"David, I am sure, has a wonderful report to give." He looked up at his mother. "I don't know how parents could have a finer son. We would like you all to come over to the house after the meeting to visit with David and have punch and cookies. I say all of these things in the name of Jesus Christ. Amen."

His mother turned and walked back to her seat. She said something to his father, who stood up. His mother had kept all of his missionary letters, and every month she had put a paragraph about him in the ward newsletter. When he became a senior companion, zone leader, and then district leader, she had put in his picture. She wrote him long encouraging letters.

His mother had been active in the Church all of her life, but he had heard her bear her testimony only at his farewell, and although they had talked often about his being good, they had never talked about the Savior, assumed everything. A testimony was easier in the mission field.

David looked up at his father. He was fifteen pounds heavier than he had been two years ago, and a little slower. He had gone on a mission to the New England States just before the Second World War. In his missionary pictures he looked young, happy, stood with his companions and converts smiling. David had read his father's missionary letters, which were full of testimony to the truthfulness of the gospel and the power of the priesthood. His father had never talked to him about knowledge and power.

His father bowed his head a little, both hands gripping the sides of the pulpit. "It *is* good to have Dave home again. As his father I have always been proud of him, and I am glad that he has been on this mission to Germany. It has been a good experience for him. I am particularly glad that he had an opportunity to go to Germany and learn German. I wanted to go to Europe on my mission."

Listening, David watched the ward. He looked again for Todd Campbell on the back rows. He would come in the next few minutes if he was coming at all. Dave sat straighter in his chair, gripped his German Bible and triple combination, rested them on his knee.

He had studied German two years at Provo High, spent two months in the LTM in Provo, and he had vowed that he would speak German perfectly, but he never had. He never had felt absolutely sure, didn't know when some German would laugh, say in English after he had spoken one sentence, "You are an American, yes?" He hated that feeling of always being capable of a stupid mistake, being embarrassed, never really ever being able to get rid of his accent.

There were elders who played chess for hours, went daily to American movies, practiced their guitars, wrote poetry, stayed in bed until late afternoon, heads covered, and then they lied when they filled out their weekly reports. They hid their scriptures from themselves. They seemed afraid of the promised power if they worked hard, afraid of what they might learn, the new possibility, afraid finally of their own real conversion. They couldn't live by faith, accept the obligations of humility; they lived only by their bodies, habit, and the love of their families, friends, and girls. They were willing to waste their lives for an honorable release because they loved home more than their priesthood or any honesty. The most intelligent of these became totally ironic, so that everything was a joke, and nothing was practical.

And some elders played mission politics, so calculated even the public prayers they spoke, wanted to be an assistant to President Maxwell. Elder Garner had said one morning, "I really need to be a senior companion, district leader, zone leader, assistant to the president, Elder Thatcher. You don't, but I do. I need to be progressing all the time in the gospel. My father is a bishop."

Elder Garner was from Los Angeles. He sent home for new American shirts, ties, and socks. He had brought five suits with him on his mission.

David sat up straighter in his chair. He pulled his shirt cuffs down half an inch. He looked at his new suit and shoes. Slowly clothes, cars, athletics, and home had become no longer so important to him and not his constant preoccupation, which was evidence of how he was changing. He wasn't as embarrassed any more. Even girls became less important. At first he was afraid of the change because of all the excitement that girls and sex meant, had meant, would mean, but then he began to see that sex didn't have to be the ultimate experience of his life.

His new feeling didn't limit him, but suggested some infinite emotion, demanded that he accept final obligation, accept all of the promises made in the scriptures. He tried to be careful about what was happening to him, love and spiritual experience as real as eating or drinking. Elder Marven, whom President Maxwell and an elders court had excommunicated for fornication, had shot himself in his father's car the first night he was home.

David looked up at *his* father. He had started to tell his missionary stories.

David slipped his hand inside his jacket and took out his talk; he opened it and read through the outline again. He had gone through his journal to find the best spiritual experiences. He rubbed his fingers over his Bible. He'd tried to write in his journal only those things that had really happened. Even in the mission field some elders used other elders' spiritual experiences as their own, bore testimony to them, made no distinction between what they had heard and what they experienced themselves, so became totally sentimental. An elder really needed the companionship of the Holy Ghost to help keep him honest. He needed to know the people in the Book of Mormon and the Bible too. They had to be real people.

His mother reached over to squeeze his arm. He smiled at her and slipped the talk back into his jacket pocket. His mother watched his father, smiled.

Three months before he had been released his mother had written to ask him what his plans were when he got home. Now everbody asked him if he would start at B.Y.U. again, what his major was, and already they wanted to know if he thought he and Jane would get married soon. He'd begun to feel that last two or three days as if his presence demanded a purity of life from his family and ward members that they did not want to give; they seemed afraid that he might ask them to believe more than they could tolerate. Ward members said, "Well, David, it will take you a month or two to come back down to earth after your mission, but you'll be okay. You need to get married."

"What do you mean?" he wanted to say, but he didn't. He had tried to be kind to everybody, be happy all of the time. Everybody seemed so comfortable, as if that was what the Church was for, and you didn't have to spend your life defining words like faith, love, humility, priesthood, and God. You had to be very careful with words.

When, after he had been in Germany three months, he had decided to find out if the gospel was true, so that he could go home if it wasn't, he began to get up even earlier than Elder Harris to study. Every new German word he learned, scripture he memorized, tract he passed out, discussion he led proved to himself how much he wanted to know if the gospel was true. But he didn't *want* it to be true then, already afraid perhaps of the obligation of knowing that, the intensity of life, the understanding. He had studied, prayed, fasted, tried by force of his own will to experience a manifestation of the Holy Ghost, use his priesthood.

All his life he had heard of missionaries fasting, praying, and then being prompted by the Holy Ghost to get off a streetcar where they had not intended to, walk up a strange street, knock on a strange door. They found a sick child near death who needed to be blessed, healed through the power of the priesthood, which always brought the whole family into the Church. At first he had hated fasting, being hungry, not being strong enough to pedal his bicycle up a hill. He didn't like the feeling of absolute weakness, didn't like depending on the spirit, praying every other hour, denying his body.

"You begin to feel it don't you, Elder Thatcher?" Elder Harris had said to him one evening four months after he had arrived in Giessen, at the end of a day of tracting.

He looked up from working the combination lock on his bicycle. "Yes," he said, and it was the first time that he had felt any love for Elder Harris, but he said nothing about that. They got on their bikes and rode down Kaiserstrasse across the cobblestones.

He told no one about what was happening to him, not his mother or father, not even Dan, Ron, and Scott, whom he wrote to every month in their circulating letter. It was too personal, the beginning of a new mind and a new heart, the feeling of beginning power, new happiness, as if he might be imagining it all. But then change had become the index of what was happening to him, proof that it was all real, which he couldn't deny.

David looked at the backs of his father's shoes; every day his father polished his shoes. On Sunday he polished everybody's shoes in the family. Sending a son on a mission could be an act of faith, repentance, love, or simply something a father did. What you had left at the end of your life was what you believed.

He listened to his father's voice. He was almost finished. He looked again for Todd Campbell. He still hadn't come in, and now he wouldn't. Starting on the back row, David began to name the faces. He knew practically every person in the congregation by name, and he knew that they didn't want him to tell them about the everyday boredom, doubt and failure, and even despair a missionary faced. Frantic, some elders boasted a testimony of Jesus Christ they didn't have, described feelings and spiritual experiences they had never earned, declared the power of the priesthood. Finally they began to lose their capacity to really know or feel anything, couldn't change, became totally sentimental, cried every time they gave a talk or bore their testimony. Other elders studied only the language, the German culture, went to plays, operas, visited all the museums, read German poetry, for they came to trust only their minds and beautiful difficult things.

Elder Marks had said to him one night after they had gone to bed, "Look, Thatcher, everybody gets by the best he can out here. Don't sweat it so much. You'll live longer."

David looked over at the priests sitting at the sacrament table. They shouldn't have to go on missions as dumb as he had been. They needed to know the good and the bad.

Elder Greenwood, his third junior companion, didn't make it back to the room on Friday of his first week out tracting (he'd had stomach trouble from the German food the whole week). When David braked his bicycle and circled back to him there in Baumenstrasse in Offenbach, he stood straddling his bicycle, tears in his eyes, already cursing. "What's wrong, Elder?"

Greenwood didn't look up, said through his teeth, "What the hell do you think?" For three days Greenwood wouldn't leave the room. Twice he packed his suitcases. He had lettered in tennis at East High School in Salt Lake and had been president of his senior class. The Gestapo had herded the distinguished men of a town into a hot room, had them tie their pant legs with their shoelaces, and then forced each man to drink a pint of castor oil, afterward kept them standing there hours in the heat.

Elders got hepatitis, ulcers, pneumonia, had nervous breakdowns, were injured and even killed riding their bicycles in the German traffic. Elders on missions in Central and South American and Korea got diseases from which some of them would suffer all of their lives. And he had seen finally that there had to be something stronger than his body, but it scared him to think about it. Slowly he had begun to feel that his garments were a protection to him, a shield against those things which could harm or destroy him.

But perhaps the worst things that could happen to a pair of elders was when they were out tracting and the old German man or woman just looked at them, listened to them say that they were representatives of the Lord Jesus Christ, yet didn't smile or speak, but slowly closed the door.

Traveling on the German trains, David had seen through the windows the walls of dark forests, and he had remembered the pictures in his freshman western civilization textbook. It would not have surprised him to see at the edge of the forest, where the fields began, a band of Goths, Vandals, or Huns standing in the shadows, their helmets, shields, and drawn swords and raised axes glinting. Wars he had never heard of, even back to the Romans, had their inscribed iron monuments in Germany. And in the German homes, for every picture of a soldier and for every relic and souvenir of war there was a story, if he asked.

And at times he hadn't wanted to obligate people, change their lives, make them different, teach them faith, repentance, the gift of the Holy Ghost, baptism, perfection, exaltation. But he came to see that only the love of Christ, belief in him, in the gospel could make the world good. The gospel wasn't sentimental; it was real, fact. He had seen it change individual converts, whole families, dozens of missionaries, and he had begun to see now what it had done to him and how it had made him new. Who promised more than Christ?

Faith made everything possible, made life infinite, and faith could become knowledge finally. The Church had twenty thousand missionaries out, and there would be in the next years thirty, forty, fifty thousand, whatever it took to spread the gospel. He knew that.

Sitting there on the stand, about to give his welcome-home talk, his father finishing now, David wondered what Elder Harris had said when he got home. He would have liked to have heard that. Elder Harris was majoring in German literature at Stanford.

"We would like you all to come and visit with Dave and have some punch and cookies." David looked up at his father. "In the name of Jesus Christ. Amen." His father turned and walked back to his chair.

Bishop Fielding stood up. "Brothers and sisters, now we come to the part of the program we have all been waiting for. But before I let Dave have the pulpit, I want to read to you part of a letter I received from his mission president. President Maxwell says here that Dave had more success tracting than almost any other elder in the Central German Mission."

All the rows of faces turned to look at him again. He had always studied each German door as he and his companion approached it. Most Germans lived in row houses. He could go to the Deseret Industries and buy back his missionary clothes. A companion wouldn't be hard to find.

"Sister Nielsen, we are missionaries of the Church of Jesus Christ of Latter-day Saints with a message of salvation for you."

She would laugh. "But, David, we *are* members of the Church. You know that."

"Yes, we know. We are bringing you a message of hope, love, humility, and compassion. We are preaching faith in Jesus Christ, repentence, and the power of the Holy Ghost. Could we set up an appointment with you? We want the whole ward to renew its faith, become truly converted to Christ. We bring you the faith we learned in the mission field where you sent us to preach the gospel. What time does Brother Nielsen come home from work? When would be the best time for an appointment? We want you to hear our testimonies."

The bishop finished reading President Maxwell's letter. It would not have surprised David to see Brother and Sister Schindler, Brother Schwartz, and Brother Binderwald, his converts, in the audience, flown over from Germany just to sit and listen to what he would say. He had found them all tracting.

"Well, Elder Thatcher, it's your turn now, the moment you waited for for two years. After Dave is finished, we'll hear a few words from the stake president."

He looked up at Bishop Fielding, who turned, walked back to his seat, and sat down. Slowly, David stood up and walked to the pulpit. He put his scriptures down on the edge of the pulpit, reached into his jacket for his outlined talk, unfolded it and laid it on the pulpit. He raised his head to look out at the congregation. Everybody smiled at him. He stood there, hands gripping the sides of the pulpit. People began to cough, move in their seats.

He glanced down at his talk. "Brothers and sisters, I want to thank you all for being here tonight. Particularly I want to thank my mother and father and my family for all of their support during my mission. I love them very much. It's good to be home again. And I pray this afternoon that I might talk under the influence of the Spirit. I want to tell you about my mission and what I learned. I know that I can't do that without the companionship of the Holy Ghost. That was one of the things I learned."

Still gripping the sides of the pulpit tight with both hands, he looked for Todd Campbell at the back. He wasn't there. David looked down at the outlined categories. People started coughing again, shifting. Reaching over with his right hand, he folded the two typed pages and slipped them back into his inside jacket pocket. He looked up at all the faces; a few people still smiled up at him. He cleared his throat, and then he began.

GREG

When Greg woke up he lay on his stomach. The shaft of sunlight coming through the window hit his gold tennis trophy, Kellie's gold-framed picture, and his clock on top of the dresser. Priesthood meeting was at nine. Greg buried his face in his pillow, closed his hands into fists and shoved them under his chest. He had promised Kellie again last night that during priesthood he would see Bishop Swensen in his office, confess what he had done, explain that she was pregnant, and ask what he had to do to repent. At ten-thirty he would pick up Kellie; they would go see her bishop, and then go tell their parents and make arrangements for the wedding that week. He tightened his fists, pushed his face deeper into the pillow. This was one of the sins you had to confess to your bishop to be forgiven of, but he knew that he still couldn't do it.

He wanted to get in his Mustang and drive as far away from Provo as he could get, say goodbye to everything and everybody. If he left he would still feel sinful all the time, no matter how often he showered and changed his clothes, but at least he wouldn't be around his family and friends, who loved him. He had prayed, tried to repent, made all kinds of promises to the Lord if only Kellie wouldn't be pregnant and he was clean again and wouldn't have to get married. But she didn't have a miscarriage. He wanted everything the way it had been. Kellie had always been popular at school.

His face in the pillow, Greg heard Kim running the shower in the hall bathroom. Kim had just turned twelve and been made a deacon; he had gotten his new suit to be ordained in and to pass the sacrament in. During the week he had just finished collecting his fast offerings for the first time, and he had his packet of blue envelopes ready to turn in this morning. They had shared the end bedroom before Steve went on his mission, and since April they had played a lot of tennis together.

Kim always said, "Hey, Greg, come on, hurry, or we won't get a court." Kim went out and sat in the Mustang to wait for him after he got home from work at Carson's Market, where he was a bagger. Like Roger and Steve, Greg had earned his Eagle Scout badge (he didn't get his Duty to God Award) and graduated from seminary. Already Kim had his First Class badge. Greg couldn't stand to think about his father and older brothers knowing about Kellie, but it was even worse if his mother and Kim knew.

Downstairs in the living room Roger's, Steve's, and his and Kim's pictures stood on the fireplace mantel, in order of age, all of them smiling (they were Roger's and Steve's missionary pictures). In his picture he was still the same as his brothers. He and Kim always went to watch Roger and Steve when they

110

played on the Provo High tennis team.

The hall phone rang three times, then stopped. Greg lifted his head out of the pillow. His mother had taken it on the kitchen extension. His father had already left for his high council meeting. He let his head sink. For three months their ringing phone stopped him, made him turn. It scared him that somebody had found out about Kellie and him and was calling to tell his mother and father. He had changed his whole life. Now sometimes he had an ache in the back of his throat and his eyes would suddenly fill with tears. He didn't ever cry, although he was afraid he would.

He tightened his jaws, pushed his face deeper into the pillow. He had to black out his mind when he started to think that people would know that he had gotten Kellie pregnant in her father's cabin in Provo Canyon. His former Primary and Junior Sunday School teachers came up to him in church to shake his hand. "Well, now that you've graduated from high school you'll be going on your mission in a year, won't you, Greg," they said. "Your parents are proud of their boys" (a miscarriage was natural).

Sundays he stood at his bedroom window and watched the neighbors walking to their meetings. He had been blessed, baptized, and confirmed in the chapel, received all of his priesthood ordinations there. He passed it every day driving up Ninth East to Kellie's. It was as if he had lied to everybody, so he couldn't be happy.

He had been named the best-dressed boy at Provo High last year, he would start at B.Y.U. next month, and he was going on his mission in a year (his father had started a mission savings account for him when he was born). But if he and Kellie got married, he might as

111

well publish an announcement in the *Herald* that she was pregnant. All the other priests in the quorum would know. Every six months Bishop Swensen talked to the quorum about chastity and the feeling of being clean. They were supposed to see Bishop Swensen if they had any problems. He would be the only married priest in the ward. He had known some of the priests in the quorum all of his life. Everybody at Provo High knew who slept around and who didn't, although it was supposed to be a secret.

One night he drove his Mustang out on the freeway at ninety miles an hour to crash into the big square cement overpass supports near the American Fork exit, a note in his shirt pocket. But he imagined himself after death as a suicide (he could actually see himself as a person), so it was stupid. He and Kellie should have gone to Reno and gotten married that first week, but they couldn't be sure that early. Because an abortion was murder he hadn't been able to even talk to Kellie about one. It would only make her more unhappy than she already was. Being married changed too many things.

He wanted to join the army and volunteer for hazardous duty somewhere, just say goodbye and go, everything simple again and in order. But he couldn't imagine his life away from his family, and Kellie, pregnant, had become somebody he shouldn't leave. Yet he couldn't stand people loving him if he didn't deserve it; he wanted to tell them not to. He felt better when he thought about all of the wrong things other people did.

Greg raised his face out of the pillow and looked at his clock. He listened to the shower. Kim had ridden with him the last three Sundays, since he had become a deacon. He would tell him he wasn't going this morning, make some excuse, and then go get Kellie to talk again. The full-length mirror on the back of the open closet door reflected his clothes, all hung in order, and his line of polished shoes. When he went downstairs on Monday mornings, his mother already had his dirty clothes in the washer. By Tuesday his fresh, ironed shirts hung in the closet and his other clean clothes were in his drawer.

"Bishop Swensen, Kellie and I have made a mistake I need to talk to you about." He pushed his face back into the pillow, grabbed his upper arms, squeezed, curled under the sheet. Every Sunday ward members sat on the foyer chairs waiting to see the bishop in his office. Whatever he planned to say, it meant the same thing. Bishop Swensen always shook his hand, complimented him; he knew the whole Swensen family. He had gone through school with David. It scared him that he had done something which changed the way he could feel.

He wanted to go on a mission (every day he saw the elders from the language training mission at B.Y.U.), graduate from college, go to dental school, live in Provo the rest of his life and raise a family, be a part of everything. Roger was in law school at Stanford, married to Stephanie, and they had Sammy, who was one now. Steve, still on his mission in Italy, was going to be an engineer. If they hadn't started going up to Kellie's father's cabin to do the yard work, nothing would have happened.

The high school biology films showed the fertilized human egg, the weekly growth of the fetus, how it grew and grew, Kellie getting bigger and bigger, which he couldn't stop, his whole life hard because of

113

just one mistake. He had planned to do a lot of different things before he got married and became a father. Kellie was great, but he hadn't thought of any girl as his wife. He wanted to have a son, hold him, feel his weight, hear his sounds, see his face, choose his name (over the front-room desk his mother had the framed family pedigree chart, little oval face pictures by some of the names).

He wanted to name his son, bless him, have his father, Roger, and Steve in the circle with him in front of the whole ward. He wanted to bear his testimony afterward about how wonderful it was to be married and have a son, an eternal family of his own, now that he was back from his mission. But it took a year to repent and be worthy, so they wouldn't make him an elder in time to bless his own son. Blessing his own son was one of the things they would take away from him. The Relief Society could help Kellie go away and have the baby, get it adopted by members, but Kellie didn't want to do that. He didn't want her to be any more unhappy than she was, even though some of it was her fault. Before, he had known exactly how his life would be.

He loosened his arms, straightened out under the sheet. He turned his head. Particles of dust floated in the bright shaft of window sunlight. After his shower he used to like to stand in the sun and lift his weights to see his body better. Now it was like he had grown scales. He wanted to stab himself in the chest with a knife until the tight feeling went away and his body was light and free again. It scared him that sometimes he wanted to live with Kellie all the time, not caring about anything else, be carnal, just let his body take over and always be that way. (In his Book of Mormon seminary class they studied repentance and what carnal meant. He felt carnal now. He knew what it meant now.)

"Greg, oh, Greg," Kellie had said when they drove back down Provo Canyon from her father's cabin, and started to cry again. Still numb with surprise at what he had done, he drove up on the B.Y.U. campus, and while they walked from one quad to the next in the darkness between the lamps, he explained *again* that nobody else had to know. As long as they repented, never did it again, tried to perfect their lives, everything was just between them and the Lord. Even though a person's sins were as red as scarlet, they would be washed away, made as white as snow, and then the Lord didn't remember them any more if the person repented. It was supposed to be a wonderful feeling.

In the Bible and the Book of Mormon, David, Paul, Alma, and the sons of Mosiah had committed sins, but they had repented, became great church leaders, some saw Christ even. He told Kellie that everything would be all right if they repented, kept clean for a year before they got married in the temple (his mission would take twice that long). They wouldn't even know that they had done something wrong, couldn't remember it, feel the pain. Their lives wouldn't be hard or complicated any more. He *liked* Kellie. He really wanted her to get married in the temple so that she could go to the celestial kingdom. It surprised him that he could only think of time as eternal. He wanted all of his good feelings back.

Every night and morning that first month he prayed on his knees for forgiveness and that Kellie wouldn't be pregnant. She couldn't be pregnant. It had really only happened just that once. He prayed over and over again in the name of Jesus Christ, prom-

115

ised that he would dedicate his whole life to the Church, go on two missions. He tried every day to be perfect in his thoughts and actions to prove that he was serious, so test the Lord. But all the time he knew that he had to confess to Bishop Swensen even if Kellie had a miscarriage, or was not even pregnant.

"Hey, Greg, you can have the shower."

He raised his head off the pillow.

"Hey, Greg."

"Okay."

Greg turned from the window and lay on his back looking up at the white ceiling. He never knew when he would have the ache in his throat, his eyes filling with tears. It was always sudden, and he had to turn away from people.

The pain was physical, a tight glowing heaviness he couldn't take medicine for. He wanted to fly, rise up above Provo, his arms wings, grow lighter and freer the higher he went until he vanished even to himself.

Once he had tried to joke with Kellie about what had happened, but that meant he didn't know how to feel anything, not right or wrong. But if he confessed, told his parents, everybody would see him as a different person. When he thought about telling his mother, he had to close his eyes. At the family reunions he uncles and older cousins held up the new babies born the past year and told their names. The whole family would know what he had done. It was as if he had made people sick or broken their bones.

In the six-month interviews with Bishop Swensen, he'd only had to confess a little fooling around, but now he felt just like the bishop said an immoral priest would (he wanted to go down into a deep mine shaft and have it cave in). Kim liked to sit with the deacons, all the deacons wearing dress shirts and ties and some of them jackets. Even if nobody told him about Kellie he would understand later.

"We have to confess, Greg," Kellie kept saying. It was as if confession were more important for her even after she knew that she was pregnant than it was for him. Even though Kellie was one of the nicest girls he'd every gone steady with, he sometimes now wanted her to vanish, dissolve, melt, so that nobody would ever know she was pregnant, his life simple again, happy.

Yet, assigned to bless the sacrament, he had to sit on his hands to keep from jumping up in front of the whole ward and shouting that Kellie was pregnant. He wanted to tell every customer at Carson's as he bagged their groceries. He wanted to write Roger and Steve, wanted to go down on his knees to tell his mother and Kim (his mother loaned him money when he needed it). He wanted there to be a movie of all the rotten things each priest in the quorum had ever done, and they would have to sit through the movies with him so that they couldn't ever laugh at him because of Kellie.

He lay there still looking up at the white ceiling, then got out of bed. He put on his robe, looked down out of the window. His Mustang glistened in the sunlight. Every Sunday men and boys walked by their house going to priesthood. He had gone to church in the ward his whole life. He raised his hands into the shaft of sunlight palms up. He didn't like to hear people were getting married or see babies or pregnant women. He had liked being twelve. Kim had the same fast offering packet he'd had, except the envelopes were blue now. He kept thinking of all the things his

117

parents had done for him.

He turned from the window. The sunlight still hit his tennis trophy and Kellie's graduation picture. "Yes," he always said when she asked him if he loved her, and he always put his arm around her shoulder. After he bought her the wedding band and took her to Salt Lake to get the test so that they would know for sure, she asked him more often. He would have to get a better job, work full-time, go to college only part-time, rent an apartment, pay bills. Kellie had always been fun, but it scared him to have to imagine his whole life with her. He didn't know how to feel.

He had to see her once more and figure out everything again. Last week they had decided to go to California; they would write their families to say goodbye, that they would be married in Nevada on the way and be back in a year. Figuring things out so much was like telling lies.

Kellie directed the singing in Junior Sunday School. Her father was in the stake Sunday School presidency, and her mother taught Primary. "Greg, it's nice to see you again," her mother always said; her little brother and two sisters wanted him to come to their family night. He pressed his forehead against the wall, closed his eyes, shoved his fists under his arms, squeezed. He wanted to phone Kellie's parents to tell them, not have to watch their faces. He never felt happy any more.

Roger and Stephanie had sent out over six hundred reception invitations, and they spent a whole day in their apartment opening wedding presents, the living room full of white tissue paper and white boxes. He and Kellie wouldn't be able to have a reception now, which was stupid.

118

He wanted to go up to Alta on a clear blue day after it had snowed all night, be the only person on the lift, not take Kim, who had skied with him all winter (Roger and Steve liked to ski Alta best). And he wanted to ski the powder to his waist, make the only trails, be surrounded by all that white, and the cloudless blue sky. And he wanted to ski and ski, the powder swirling up around him, feel only the smoothness and absolute control of skiing, ski until he remembered nothing but white. His new Lange boots were a Christmas present from his parents last year.

Standing there, Greg opened his eyes and moved his forehead from contact with the wall. He held his tingling hands under his arms. He had wanted to smash his hands against the rock wall of Kellie's father's cabin. He couldn't stay busy enough not to think. He had tried to change the feeling alone. The Lord needed to be somebody he could phone or go to his office to see.

In seminary they had discussed how a person could become dead to all righteousness, his life stopped, if he didn't repent so the Lord could help him. He wanted to lose all memory of what he had done wrong and not feel anything. They had only done it once, not over and over again every day, which would have been like everything getting darker.

"Greg?" His mother knocked. "It's after eight. You don't want to be late for priesthood. Breakfast is almost ready."

Greg turned to face the door. "Okay, Mom."

"Don't fall back to sleep, son."

"Okay, Mom."

His mother called Kim and then walked back down the hall. After he had taken Kellie home that night and

119

got her to stop crying, he wanted to drive down to the Provo Cold Storage Plant, go in the big room where their locker was, and freeze, stop the feeling. He wanted everybody to have done something wrong.

Greg opened his door and walked across the hall to the bathroom. Kim's wet footprints showed on the tile floor and beads of water ran down the shower walls. Kim had gone back three times to collect the Snyders' fast offering. He wore his new clothes only on Sunday (with his birthday money he had bought shoes, socks, tie, and shirt to go with his new suit). He always stopped in the chapel foyer to look at Steve's and the other missionaries' pictures. When they turned twelve, their birthday present from their parents was the new suit.

Greg turned on the shower hard to let the water beat against the top of his head and face. He would tell Kim that he had a headache. His mother would leave right after breakfast for her Sunday School inservice meeting. He closed his eyes. He didn't like to shower any more; he wanted his body always covered with layers of clothes. (He kept trying to remember what it was like to be twelve and have the priesthood new.) He had to force himself to play tennis with Kim.

After he took Kellie home, he drove around for two hours before he parked in the driveway (he had driven by Bishop Swensen's house three times). He sat in the Mustang and looked at his parents' bedroom window, rested his head against the steering wheel, the ache coming in his throat, but he didn't cry. He wanted to ring the doorbell and ask if he could come in. He showered, soaped his body again and again that night, but there wasn't enough soap and hot water in the world to make him happy. The next morning he showered again, turned the shower on full-force cold to numb his body and mind, wore all clean clothes, polished his shoes again, but he couldn't change how his body felt.

He couldn't stop thinking about the biology film, the human egg already growing if it was fertilized. He wanted to pull a lever to make everything again like it had been. He didn't have any right even to say goodbye. He wanted repentance to feel great and then to tell everybody about it.

The hall phone rang again. Greg opened his eyes and turned down the shower. He wanted to press his whole body against the cool tile wall. The phone stopped. His mother always started Sunday dinner before she left for Sunday School.

He had been terrified of going downstairs to breakfast the first morning because he thought that his parents and Kim would know just by looking into his face what he had done. "Son," his father had said as they knelt around the table by their chairs for family prayer, "it's your turn." The tablecloth touching his cheek, he had prayed, stunned that he could because he was lying, expected to be struck dumb, but he hadn't been. (His mother ran the boat when the family went waterskiing.)

He met Kellie after every class they didn't take together, held both her hands, put his arm around her shoulder. And it amazed him that none of their friends stopped and said, "What's wrong with you two? You're different." He practiced with the tennis team, showered, talked to his teachers. He saw kids who had reputations for sleeping around. He didn't want anybody to think that about him or Kellie. Girls had dropped out of school during the year because they got pregnant. The night he and Kellie graduated he watched the face of every person who walked across the stage to get a diploma.

In seminary they had learned that to be carnally minded was death. The pioneers used to stand up in meetings and confess all of their sins to the ward. After the first month, every day he waited for Kellie to phone him and say she'd had a miscarriage, so they wouldn't have to get married. Her mother baked him a birthday cake; her little brother and sisters bought him a present. He had ruined it all. Stupid.

Blessing the sacrament was the hardest thing he did. That first Sunday when he stood to break the bread into the silver trays, he thought that Bishop Swensen would suddenly stand up in front of the whole ward and say into the microphone, "No, Greg, stop. You shouldn't bless the sacrament." The silver bread trays glinted in the sunlight as the deacons carried them from row to row under the windows. He blessed the water. His mother, Kim, and the whole ward looked up at him and the other two priests (his father had a high council assignment).

Sitting at the sacrament table, he had put his hands under his arms and squeezed against the pain. The Relief Society washed and ironed the linen sacrament cloths. He had lost the feeling for blessing the sacrament, singing hymns, listening to prayers, hearing talks and lessons. When he was a deacon he would open his eyes to watch Roger's face when he blessed the sacrament. Even the meaning of words had changed. He needed to jump off a cliff, but keep falling, fall off the world, just have the sensation forever. Reaching up, he turned off the shower and got out.

122

In his room, he combed his hair first, and then started to dress. He'd always liked the feel of a fresh long-sleeved dress shirt against his skin; sometimes he didn't wear a jacket so that he could feel the shirt. His mother bought him new clothes for Christmas and his birthday. He kept a wax shine on his Mustang because of the feeling. Sitting on the edge of his bed, he put on his polished shoes. He put on his watch and dug for a handkerchief in his drawer. He was afraid of crying.

An abortion or Kellie going away to have the baby so that it could be adopted by a member family seemed simple, sometimes. He looked up at Kellie's picture. He didn't drive by the temple now unless he had to. At night, illuminated, the temple was almost white. He and Kellie had only done it once, but he felt like he had burned down the house or something. What he had done seemed written down. He and Kellie had always had their own set of rules about what was wrong for them to do.

"Hey, Greg, you ready?" His door opened and Kim stuck just his head in. "Mom said to hurry. It's eight-thirty."

He looked at his clock. "Go ahead. Tell Mom I'll be down in a minute."

"Okay, but hurry." Kim closed the door. He didn't put on his jacket until after he ate. Kim shined his new shoes every Sunday; they were just like Greg's newest pair.

Greg combed his hair again in the dresser mirror. The sun had left Kellie's picture and his tennis trophy. He would eat first and then tell Kim he wasn't going; his mother would think that he wasn't feeling well. Kim would be disappointed. Already Kim looked forward to saying one of the prayers at his missionary farewell, next spring. Kim and he had said the prayers at Steve's farewell, and Roger had flown out from Stanford to speak.

But there wouldn't be any farewell for him now. The other priests in the quorum would go on missions, have their pictures in the chapel foyer, learn foreign languages, convert people, but the Church wouldn't let him go. Roger, who had gone to Germany, had been a first assistant to his mission president. Greg put his comb in his pocket. He didn't like to see the groups of missionaries from the language training mission; they were happy; they did something.

He didn't turn from the mirror. He wanted Bishop Swensen to have a big book in the office with all of his awards, certificates, Scout badges listed, the tithing he had paid, all of the hours he had spent working on the stake welfare farm, at the cannery, and with his attendance at all the meetings he had been to all his life. And he wanted the bishop to say, "Well, Greg, I will just cross off your Eagle badge, your seminary graduation, and all your tithing to pay for what you have done. Now the Lord forgives you. You don't have to worry about Kellie or the baby, or get married. You can go on your mission. You will feel clean like you were before, and Kellie is a nice girl."

Just that one mistake cancelled out all the good that he had ever done. He would have to start all over if he stayed in Provo. A carnal person's body was different from a good person's; he felt and understood things in a different way. He couldn't change back, really repent, unless he went to his bishop so the Lord could help him. Greg turned from the mirror. He'd stopped praying three weeks ago. He couldn't believe that his mother and father or brother had ever done anything really wrong (Kim was too young).

He walked to his door, opened it and went down the hall. He stopped at the head of the stairs and turned to look back at the family pictures on the wall. Some of the family lines connected to Bible genealogy and went clear back to Adam. In the resurrection a person had a bright recollection of all of his unrepented sins and knew everybody else's unrepented sins.

At the bottom of the stairs he stopped again. Kim was talking to his mother. His father was gone to his meeting. He turned and looked at the front door. He could get in his Mustang and drive away, pick up Kellie; he would just leave a note saying goodbye. Sunday had always been a relaxed good day. Everybody was happier and kinder on Sunday.

Kellie would be in maternity clothes for at least five months. Sunday after Sunday he would have to sit next to her in church, and every week she would be a little bigger. Even if they lived in another Provo ward after they got married, some people would know about them, and feel sorry for them and their families. But people couldn't ask when the baby would be born. Both his and Kellie's families were among the most active in their wards. He walked down the hall. Sammy had received a lot of presents when he was born.

"Hey, Greg, come on. We'll be late. I already said the blessing."

"Oh." He sat down, spread his napkin on his lap, and drank half his orange juice. Kim had his tie tucked inside his shirt while he ate. On Sundays they had family prayer at dinner, when his father was home.

"Good morning, son."

"Good morning, Mom," he said, but he didn't look above the level of the gleaming white stove and dishwasher.

"How many eggs do you want this morning, Greg?"

He raised his head. His mother, two eggs in her right hand, held the refrigerator door open. "I'm not very hungry. I'll just eat some cereal." The top door shelf was full of eggs.

"Don't you feel well, son?"

"I'm okay, I guess."

"Would you like something else?" His mother closed the refrigerator door.

"No, thank you."

He poured milk on one shredded wheat biscuit, cut it with his spoon. He looked up at his mother, who faced the cupboards. The heavy knife lay on the sideboard by the half loaf of homemade bread. Yesterday when he was adjusting the timing on the Mustang, he had wanted to push his hands into the whirling fan, afterwards walk into the kitchen and show his mother, tell her about Kellie then.

"The deacons quorum is going to plan a swimming party to Saratoga, Greg."

He closed his eyes, tightened his jaws. Roger and Steve would shake his hand, put an arm around his shoulder, and ask him what they could do to help, say that they loved him. He would want to explain how it all happened, how one thing just led to another; how did he tell them that it only happened once? He pushed back his chair, stood up. "I guess I wasn't even as hungry as I thought. Excuse me."

"Are you sure you're all right, son? You've looked

126

a little pale lately."

"I'll go brush my teeth."

"Now, Kim, you sit there and finish your breakfast. You don't have to be running after Greg every minute."

"Ah, Mom, isn't Greg going to priesthood?"

After he had brushed his teeth and combed his hair, he stood by his window looking down at the street. Jeff Walker and his dad passed along going to priesthood, Brother Cory behind them. Greg looked over at his clock. If he confessed to Bishop Swensen today and married Kellie during the week, next Sunday the whole quorum would know. He would be the only married priest. If the bishop let him meet with the elders, he would be with all the married returned missionaries, all of them married in the temple. When they brought their first new babies to church, they kept bending down to kiss them all through the meeting. Roger had sent Sammy's hospital picture and Greg's mother had a miniature made for the family pedigree chart hanging in the front room.

"Greg." He turned from the window. Kim stood in the doorway.

"Hey, Greg, it's time to go. Aren't you going?" He carried his packet of blue fast-offering envelopes in his right hand.

Greg turned. More men and boys walked to priesthood; two cars went by. Later, mothers and fathers would pass taking their children to Sunday School, and then in the afternoon again whole families would be going to sacrament meeting.

"Greg, you feel all right don't you?"

In priesthood meeting, the priests sat together on the right side of the chapel. Bishop Swensen always stopped to shake hands with each priest and ask him if he'd had a good week and if he was happy. Greg turned back to Kim, who had walked into the room. The closet door mirror held both of them.

"Let's go, Greg."

He looked at their shoes. He turned from the mirror to look at Kim. He was smiling. (Kim had asked him to go with him to buy his new shoes at Clark's so he would be sure to get the same kind.) Greg walked slowly to the closet and got his blue blazer. "I'll be okay, I guess," he said. As he put on the blazer he looked at Kellie's picture.

"Great," Kim said.

He followed Kim down the stairs. In the hall he stopped before the mirror. He buttoned the blazer and then felt to see that he had his handkerchief.

"Goodbye, son!"

Greg stopped on the porch, turned, saw his mother framed in the hallway, but he did not speak. He turned slowly and walked down the front steps, the storm door closing behind him.

Kim already sat in the Mustang; he had the windows rolled down. Greg backed out and drove down the street. Kim had him stop to pick up Brian Madsen and David Tuttle, two deacons who were walking. They had their fast-offering packets. "You guys get all your fast offerings collected?" Kim asked.

"Sure."

"Sure."

"So did I."

Greg watched the car ahead of them slow down to turn into the chapel parking lot.

"Good," he said.

TESTIMONY

Holding the song book up for Helen, but not singing, Glen looked over the rows of heads at Eric, who sat at the sacrament table between the Terry and Strong boys. Eric held the song book; all three boys sang. Glen had ordained Eric a priest earlier that morning, and now Eric would bless the sacrament for the first time. Hands on Eric's head, in the name of Jesus Christ and by the authority of the holy Melchizedek priesthood, he had blessed Eric that he would always be receptive to the promptings of the Holy Ghost, keep himself morally clean, prepare himself to go on a mission, study hard in school, love his younger brothers and sisters, and be protected.

"I bless you," he said, "now that you have your driver's license, that you will obey all the traffic laws and drive safely." As he spoke the blessing, Eric's thick brown hair grew warm, and Glen raised his hands a little, the other hands on top of his, so that the weight wouldn't be uncomfortable on Eric's head. Eric wore his hair as long as Glen would let him, his hair thick and brown like Helen's. People were always

129

saying how much Eric looked like both of them.

"Thanks, Dad," Eric said after the ordination, and shook hands with him, Bishop Simmons, and the others in the circle. But Eric didn't stand and bear his testimony in the short testimony meeting the bishop had held in the priest class as part of fast Sunday. He didn't have to say that he knew the gospel was true, but just stand up and say that he appreciated the Church, loved the family, loved his mother, felt he was blessed, lucky to live in Provo, anything, just so he wanted to do it out of himself, but Eric just sat there looking down at his new shoes.

"Well, son," he wanted to say, "you're sixteen now. What do you believe?"

"He's a fine boy, Glen," Bishop Simmons said after the priest class was over, put his hand on Glen's shoulder.

Glen had gone to four or five of Eric's Explorer basketball games that winter, and each time it surprised him how tall Eric was, his body shining with sweat. Girls shouted his name when he made a basket, and after the game before he went to the showers, talking to him, they reached out to touch him. One flashy little blonde reached up to run her fingers through his hair.

For the last six months, maybe a year, Glen had sensed that Eric was moving away from him, that he no longer really influenced Eric's life much (he saw Eric only at breakfast, maybe for half an hour in the evening; Eric was always on the run, going somewhere—to some friend's to study, to play ball, to some school or ward activity, out with some girl—never had five minutes to stay home.)

He wanted Eric to stay in the Church, have a strong

testimony, believe, go on a mission, go to college, get married in the temple, live by those values. He couldn't understand how Eric could live any other way and still have a life that meant anything. He wanted Eric to know that it was all true so that he would be safe. He wanted to know what kind of a life Eric would have.

He wanted Eric to bear his testimony now this morning in testimony meeting so that Eric himself would know that he believed. And Helen deserved to hear that testimony, and his grandmothers, and everybody in the ward who had ever taught him in Primary, Sunday School, priesthood, or ever worked with him in Scouting or Exploring. They deserved to know that it all meant something to him. Eric was the oldest grandson on either side of the family, the best the family could do, and the best the ward could do too, whether he knew it or not.

"Son, why don't you bear your testimony this Sunday in fast meeting. It would mean a lot to your mother. Your becoming a priest is a special day for her." All week he had wanted to put his hand on Eric's shoulder and say that, but he hadn't. If he had to tell Eric, the whole thing would be meaningless.

He had decided to bear his own testimony this morning to encourage Eric, and to let him know what *he* believed. He hadn't borne his testimony very often, perhaps not in the past five years, not since he blessed Carie. Sitting there holding the song book for Helen, singing, he saw Art Johnson, Sid Baker, Al Peterson, others, men he had lived in the ward with for ten years, who were active, had active families, men who never bore their testimonies.

Kirsten and Carie sat between their mother and

131

two grandmothers, and Bob sat with the deacons. Eric's grandmothers had come to see him bless the sacrament for the first time. Glen sang the last verse of "Come, Come, Ye Saints." Sister Lund's white baton swept in wider arcs as she tried to get the ward to feel the song, come with her. She always made a special effort to get the Aaronic priesthood boys who sat on the benches in front of the sacrament table to sing. Some Sunday mornings she stopped in the middle of a song to get them more books. He liked to sing the songs on Sunday. Even as a boy he had liked to sing, but he didn't have much of a voice.

During the opening prayer traffic noises came in through the two open side doors at the front of the chapel. The air conditioning wasn't working again. The front end of their new red Torino was just visible through the open door on the left side. Eric had parked it where everybody in the ward would see it when they walked out of the chapel. All of Eric's friends had been over to see it. The sun was a weak glow through the milky windows down both sides of the chapel. The two hornets still crawled on the top pane of the left middle window.

After the prayer Bishop Simmons stood up again, and the latecomers moved down both aisles looking for seats. The Bills dragged their seven kids down to the very front as usual, where they could make the most noise. "The first baby to be blessed this morning, brothers and sisters, is the son of Brother and Sister Melvin K. Thompson." The two babies to be blessed and the three boys to be confirmed meant less time for testimonies. The bishop had made a lot of announcements.

Eric sat straight. His new suit had six-inch-wide

132

lapels, and bell-bottomed pants like a sailor's. Last Monday, his birthday, Eric had come to the office at 9 o'clock, and Glen had driven him over to the city and county building to take his driver's test. Eric had taken the Provo High driver education course, passed the written part of the state test with only two mistakes, and Glen had changed their car insurance to cover a teenage driver.

But all week he had felt tense, scared, a surge of fear going through him if the phone rang while Eric was out with the car, kept thinking about Eric's having a license. In a split second, even within sight of the house, Eric could mangle or kill himself, change all of their lives, mangle and kill people he didn't even know or had never seen before. Two of his friends had been killed last year in a head-on.

He had given Eric the promised set of keys to the new Torino for his birthday, touched his hand; however, a moving violation would cost him his driving privileges for a month.

"I know, I know," Eric had said, holding the new keys for the first time, feeling them with his fingers.

"I hope you do, son."

Glen glanced at Helen, who watched Eric. Kirsten and Carie were still quiet. His and Helen's mothers had finally stopped whispering to each other. Bob and some of the other deacons and teachers already leaned forward to rest their foreheads on top of the next bench, as if suffering.

The women watched Thompson carry his son down the aisle, his father and father-in-law following him.

Yesterday at the office Les had told him about a sixteen-year-old nephew whose girl friend was pregnant. "Sixteen," Les said. "And do you know where it happened? In front of the TV in the family room. And it wasn't just once either. I tell you, Glen, the kids today are something. I'm glad my three are all raised and married. You can't know what a kid today will try next.''

Every week he heard horror stories about Provo teenagers, even the junior-high-school kids now, taking drugs, pushing drugs, drinking, having wild parties, sex a long series of experiments. Kids tried everything there was to try today, dropped out of school, out of the Church, out of life, destroyed their bodies and themselves. Not love, religion, family, or anything else was strong enough to hold some of them, show them what life was supposed to be.

When he was growing up in the old Provo Sixth Ward, kids had been satisfied; there weren't so many dangers, and a kid's friends weren't stronger than his family. A boy could go to hell almost overnight now.

The circle formed for blessing the baby, and the ward hushed to hear Thompson speak into the mike held up for him: "Our Father in heaven, by the authority of the holy Melchizedek priesthood which we bear and in the name of Jesus Christ, we take this infant into our arms to give him a name and a father's blessing . . .''

Helen put her hand on Glen's knee and he covered it with his. Sixteen years ago this month he had and blessed Eric, held Eric's body in his two hands. His own body heavy with love for his wife and son, that sense of family, a first child, he had blessed Eric's hands, feet, mouth, eyes, brain, and heart that he might grow up without infirmities, always be protected, and always be true to the Church, willed his son's flesh and blood to obey. He had baptized and confirmed Eric, blessed him then, blessed him when he ordained him a deacon, a teacher, blessed him today.

But he had administered to Eric, and the other kids, only when Helen suggested it. And they didn't have family prayer, except the blessing at supper sometimes became a kind of family prayer. And he had never done any of his genealogy; he took Helen to the temple maybe three or four times a year if she hinted often enough. He didn't know the standard works because he had never really studied them. He didn't bear his testimony.

He could visualize God the Father but not Jesus Christ, although now finally he began to see the need for some kind of redemption. He believed in life after death, yet he never really desired to be a god, gain the highest degree of the celestial kingdom, be exalted. He was satisfied if he could stay out of jail, get the kids decently raised, make Helen happy. But he wanted Eric to believe it all.

He looked up at Eric again. Eric had borne his testimony once, when he was eight. Each child in the Sunday School class, prompted by the teacher because they had all been recently baptized, stood up in turn to say that he knew the gospel was true, then sat down again to be giggled at and punched. Eric was active in the Explorer post, but he didn't want to get his Eagle Scout badge. They would be lucky if he got his Duty to God Award.

After Thompson finished blessing his son, he held him up for the whole ward to see, and the women turned to smile and nod to one another, the noise picking up again. "The second baby to be blessed this morning is the new daughter of Brother and Sister Richard K. Carter, Jenifer." Carter blessed the baby and then held her up, all dressed in pink. Bishop Simmons announced the names of the Mitchell, Swensen, and Jones boys, who had been baptized and were to be confirmed by their fathers. The ward clerk brought his chair over for the boys to sit on.

His and Helen's mothers were smiling. He had baptized Eric, and the Sunday he confirmed him, had given him the gift of the Holy Ghost to be his companion, guide, conscience, and protector forever. His mother had brought the twenty-year-old baptism pictures to the special dinner they had for Eric and showed how much he and Eric looked alike at eight in their white baptismal clothes.

Glen looked around at all of the women in the congregation, two or three for every man. The Church was natural for women, absolutely necessary, how they saw life. Women held a ward together. If a man had the natural faith a woman had, he could do anything. The women's section of the choir was always two to three times as big as the men's. Some women tried to hound their husbands into heaven (Valerie Wilson bore her testimony every fast Sunday, Stan, who never bore his, sitting there), which was something Helen had never done.

"Brother David Stanley Mitchell, by the authority of the holy Melchizedek priesthood in us vested . . ."

He wanted Eric to go on a mission, and he wished that he had gone himself. The draft wouldn't take him because of his eyes, and his father didn't care if he went on a mission or not, although he said he would pay if he did. His mother had been sick that year. So he hadn't had to tract eight hours a day, week after week, have doors slammed in his face, get shouted down and cursed in street meetings. And he hadn't preached, healed, prayed and fasted, used the power of the Holy Ghost, seen people converted, hadn't seen how the Church changed their lives. Not having those experiences had made a difference all of his life.

They had got Eric to start a missionary savings account, but he spent most of his money on new clothes and now girls. (A year ago he and the Nelson kid had been picked up down at Clark's for shoplifting ties, which they wanted for the Valentine's dance.) A mission was the farthest thing from some of his friends' minds. They dragged Eric away from his studies, wore their hair long, dressed a little wild, and were only out for a good time.

The Mitchell boy's father, Bishop Simmons, and the others in the circle shook hands with him after the confirmation. The Swensen boy sat in the chair and bowed his head.

The hornets had left the high window now, swung low over the Aaronic priesthood boys. The boys turned up their faces to watch the hornets, pointing, whispering, hoping they would sting somebody and cause a commotion, wouldn't fly out through one of the open doors. The hornets went looping off, rising higher toward the vaulted ceiling, rising above the chandeliers, the kids quieting down again, disappointed, bowing their heads for the confirmation.

Glen watched Bob, his head bowed, reach over to punch the Keith kid. Listening to Swensen give his son the gift of the Holy Ghost, bless him, Glen turned to look up at Eric again. In spite of everything their parents did, some kids grew up today believing that life was just one long X-rated movie. Provo boys ran away to places like San Francisco and Los Angeles, got hepatitis, gonorrhea, and they became theives, beggars, homosexuals to get money for drugs. Allen Smith had committed Brent to the State Hospital in May because of drugs, changed the family's life.

The newspapers, magazines, TV, and movies dealt with practically nothing but world pollution, population explosion, world starvation, the possibility of biological and atomic warfare, and how long God had been dead. Twice in the last year he had been invited to join neighborhood protection groups. Some men had a gun for every member of the family, had taught their children to shoot, and their year's supply of food and other essentials included a case of ammunition. Mark Henderson had his whole family taking karate.

After the second confirmtion, everybody straightened up, the coughing and whispering starting again. Hand on his son's shoulder, Swensen walked him up the aisle. On every row men were taking off their suit coats. Outside, the red Torino glimmered in the sun. The Jones boy sat in the chair and the circle closed around him.

The picture of Joseph Smith on the wall above the organ had turned to a mirror in the sunlight. Glen had looked at it every Sunday for twelve years. In October their new house in Indian Hills would be finished. Full of B.Y.U. professors, lawyers, businessmen, and dentists, their new stake was one of the two or three most active in the whole Church. The schools were better (the new high school would be up that way), and it would give Eric a chance for some new friends, boys whose parents saw that they studied, earned scholarships, went on to college.

Ten years ago they had had a chance to transfer to

California with the company, but they had decided not to take the promotion and to stay in Provo. Saturday he had heard of another Los Angeles doctor who had moved his family to Provo and then commuted once a month. The only bad thing about their move to Indian Hills was that it took Eric farther away from town, where he could get a job now. Glen had started washing dishes in the B and B Cafe when he was thirteen. But now the federal government wouldn't allow a boy to work until he was sixteen. Hell.

Eric turned his head, and his glasses reflected the diffused sunlight. He had warned Eric every day to obey all traffic laws, wear his seat belt and shoulder strap, drive defensively (Glen had for the past three months tried to obey every traffic law; he had studied the state driver's manual at his office), but all the time he knew that Eric probably had no useful concept of speed, injury, or death, would have to learn that, if he was lucky.

Eric was already talking about saving his money for a motorcycle. Nearly every kid under twenty-five who was killed in the county died in a motorcycle or car accident. When Glen showed Eric the report of an accident in the *Herald*, pointed to the pictures of smashed cars and blanket-covered bodies, he said, "Ya, one of the guys told me about it."

The parents always used a high school yearbook picture for the obituary, sometimes the son or daughter in a cap and gown. Glen closed his eyes against the image of a state trooper, hat in hand, ringing his doorbell, Bishop Simmons standing beside the trooper. Eric had been reported three times this past year for cutting classes. "Ah, we just went for a ride was all. Is that so bad?"

139

"Where did you go?"

"Oh, gad, we just went to Salt Lake and back."

"You call driving to Salt Lake on a school afternoon just going for a ride? Well, buster, you're grounded for a week. You don't go anywhere."

He had long ago passed the point when he could imagine life without Helen or the kids. He wanted the Church's idea of the eternal family to be true.

"It's wonderful, brothers and sisters, to see new babies blessed and children confirmed members of the Church." Glen opened his eyes. Bishop Simmons stood at the pulpit again. "We will now prepare ourselves to partake of the sacrament. The sacrament song is number two hundred and one, 'There Is A Green Hill Far Away.' " Glen looked up at the clock and then at his watch. They were running about twelve minutes late.

People coughed, opened their books. Sister Lund waited, her baton raised, until all the deacons, teachers, and priests had opened their song books and held them up. Eric had been in her Mother's Day Aaronic priesthood chorus. Glen had tried to pick out Eric's voice, wondering all the time how Sister Lund had ever talked him into singing.

"Eric has a nice voice," she had said. Glen held up the song book for Helen. Every fall Sister Lund invited him to join the choir, but he couldn't read music, so he never joined.

Glen felt his heart begin to pound when Eric stood and bent to break the bread into the chrome trays this first time. Eric was the tallest of the three priests. Sometimes Glen couldn't remember when he had touched him last. When Eric was little he liked to wrestle with him, let him ride on his back, liked to

140

bathe him, help him put on his pajamas, kneel with him to say his prayers.

For once there wasn't a "Wonder Bread" or "Peter Pan" wrapper visible on top of the sacrament table. Two or three rows back a baby was crying, but it stopped just before the sacrament song ended. And the whole ward was absolutely quiet finally, hushed, heads bowed. The Terry kid knelt to bless the bread, and Glen, head bowed, his heart slowing down a little (Eric would bless the water), listened for *"body."* A kid *had* to sense something when he blessed the sacrament, used his priesthood.

Glen watched Eric take his piece of bread from the chrome tray held out to him. The deacons were serious as they passed the sacrament. In the kitchen they laughed, talked about sports, bumped into the teachers as they filled the water trays from the tap, spilling the trays. And after the meeting they ate the leftover sacrament bread, and they threw the used cups at each other, hollering and laughing. He had gone into the kitchen about once a month to collar Eric. Glen took his piece of bread, held the tray for Helen, who took it and then turned to help the girls and pass it to her mother.

Glen chewed his piece of bread, sensed it begin to vanish in his mouth, without swallowing. The picture of Joseph Smith, who had seen the Father and the Son, was still a mirror. He chewed. God the Father had always been a reality, necessary to the order of the universe, the source of all law from the Ten Commandments on down. But a Christ was necessary too if you believed in justice, right and wrong, because somebody had to pay. But he didn't feel anything for Christ. He tried every Sunday when he took the sac-

141

rament to imagine Him, yet all he saw was the picture of Jesus that used to hang in the old Sixth Ward Junior Sunday School room.

He wanted to bear a testimony of Christ for Helen, his mother, her mother, the whole family, everybody in the ward, but today mostly for Eric. He wanted to say he knew that Christ lived, was the son God, and that everything was true. It was something he hadn't earned, but at times he thought that if he just said he knew, then it would be true for him. Eric would have that wherever he was. The last of the melted bread slipped down his throat.

The deacons walked back down the aisles. He took Helen's hand. Eric knelt, disappeared above the deacons' heads. His voice filled the chapel, amplified through the mike, blessing the water for all of them, giving them the chance to pledge themselves to the Savior for another week. Glen squeezed his eyes tighter shut, listened for the word "blood," which Eric might confuse with "body," have to start over. Glen opened his eyes. His dark brown hair shining in the glow of sunlight coming through the high milky windows, Eric rose above the two lines of standing deacons. Helen turned to shush Carie, and then took her hand away from under Glen's to get her handkerchief out of her purse.

Glen's heart began to slow down a little. Both of Eric's grandmothers smiled up at him. (Glen hoped that Bob would be as tall as Eric.) The ward waited for each priest to stand up on his own some fast Sunday and bear his testimony for the first time, and so tell them that it had somehow all been worthwhile, that his life would mean something.

He wanted Eric to have that sense of congregation,

believing what others believed, knowing what they would do, feel safe, realize how much that meant. Life meant more in a town like Provo. But Eric had to feel that himself and know how important it was. Glen watched the men who were bishops, high councilors, stake presidents. They seemed to grow, had emotions and understandings he didn't have, power. He was assistant to the ward Sunday School president, which was about what he deserved.

He tried to sense what other men believed, what kept them active, what they really felt, whether or not they did it because of family, social pressure, heritage, business, habit, or because they believed. He always listened to other men sing. The two hornets had dropped down to circle low over the front rows. People followed the hornets with their eyes, slowly turned their heads, tried to will them to fly out through one of the open side doors.

A deacon, Chad Williams's boy, handed Glen the tray. He drank the warm chlorinated water from the little paper cup (in memory of the blood of Christ), water dripping on his knee from the tray. Girls that Glen didn't know or had never heard of called Eric at ten and eleven at night now, and Eric was anxious to be able to take the car at night just to see a girl for a few minutes. He had known for over a year that girls liked him, thought he was good looking.

"Ah, Dad," he said, "they're just girls."

"Maybe, but girls that called boys on the phone when I was in high school were considered wild. Just tell your girl friends not to call here after ten because you won't be answering."

"But they'll think I'm just a kid."

"You're sixteen, which means that you've still

143

got a year or two left yet."

Kids today went to every extreme—free love, homosexuality, perversion of every kind—so it wasn't just a fear of Eric's getting some girl pregnant; he could become another person, which happened now to perfectly decent kids from good homes. He couldn't imagine what something like that would do to Helen. If the Church just kept Eric from drinking and smoking, kept him away from drugs, and kept him moral, then he wouldn't ask any more than that. It would be worth all of the ward budget, fast offering, and tithing he had ever paid, or would pay.

"You've got your work cut out for you, Glen, raising a kid these days," people said. "The next two or three years will be the hardest. You haven't seen anything yet."

Glen looked up at Eric again, who sat straight, watching the deacons pass the trays. In another year Eric would be as tall as he was, and probably stronger. Eric had gone out for wrestling last year, and had taken a karate class this summer offered at B.Y.U. He worked out with his weights every day. Shirtless, he stopped before every mirror in the house. A boy growing strong changed things because you couldn't touch him. Harold Banks's son Karl had grabbed Harold one night when they were having an argument about his long hair, pushed him out of the bedroom and slammed the door in his face.

Stan Tibbs's boy had stolen the neighbor's car, and, in a hundred-mile-an-hour chase with with the state highway patrol, smashed the car through a guardrail and the chain-link fence to kill himself. The guardrail had been fixed, but not the fence. Every trip to Salt Lake, Glen saw it, the skid marks where he went off, the tire ruts where he hit the first time before he started to roll. Glen watched the freeway now for skid marks, torn out guardrails and dividers, burned patches, and at night he watched ahead for the pulsing red lights.

Down at the front of the chapel Bills stood up with his baby, walked past the deacons lined up to return the trays, the baby screaming all the way to the foyer, the sound gradually fading. Glen smiled a little. When Eric was a baby and started to fuss, he had usually been grateful for the chance to take him out and so not have to listen to the speaker. He had liked to hold Eric in church, feel the warmth and heaviness of his body, watch him fall asleep.

Now in two years Eric would be out of high school. They hadn't gone on enough camping, hunting, and fishing trips together, just the two of them. He had always wanted to own a small business so that he and Eric could work together, know each other. All the small family businesses were being taken over by the big chain outfits. How did a father get to know a son he was hardly ever with?

Last November Eric and the Harris and Nelson kids had broken a window to get into the wardhouse to play basketball in the gym. Now the Nelson kid had a car of his own and tried to pull Eric off on Sunday to go fishing, boating, hiking, anything just to get out of church.

"But, Dad," Eric said, "it'll just be one Sunday."

"Your place on Sunday is in church, son. You know that as well as I do."

"But it's so boring. All the guys say it's boring."

"Maybe, but as long as you put your feet under my table you go to your meetings."

145

"Nuts. What's one Sunday going to hurt anything?"

Nowadays a kid's friends were more important than his family. He had to practically handcuff Eric to his desk every night while school was on to get him to study.

The deacons filed down the aisles to the waiting priests, the chrome trays flashing light. People stirred again, coughed. More men took off their suit coats in the growing heat.

"We want to thank the Aaronic priesthood for the fine way in which they took care of the sacrament this morning." Bishop Simmons stood at the pulpit again. "We particularly want to thank Eric Miller, whose father ordained him a priest this morning, and who blessed the sacrament for the first time. You did a fine job, Eric."

The deacons returned to the two front benches, and the three priests walked down off the stand. The Terry and Strong boys sat with the other priests, but Eric walked up the aisle toward them. He stopped, Glen pushed over to make room, and Eric sat down beside him. Helen put her hand through Glen's arm, and Glen knew he had that surprised look on his face. He wanted to put his arm around Eric's shoulders and hug him, but if he did Eric might get up and leave. The last of the latecomers made it. Eric hadn't sat with them in six weeks. He sat with either his friends or some girl.

"And now we come to the part of the meeting when we have the opportunity to bear our testimonies. I know, my dear brothers and sisters, that God lives and that his son, Jesus Christ, died for us all. I know that Joseph Smith restored the true gospel of

Christ to the earth and that a living prophet guides us today. My family and I have been truly blessed by the gospel, and we see the hand of the Lord in our lives every day. The time is now yours to bear your testimonies. The two deacons will bring the traveling microphones up the aisles to you if you will just raise your hand."

More than half of the deacons and teachers looked up at the wall clock; they were already thinking about dinner. The meeting was running about twenty minutes late, which meant only forty minutes for testimonies.

Glen watched Eric. Larry Hammond's boy came up the aisle with the mike, but Eric didn't raise his hand. "Brothers and sisters, I want to bear my testimony this morning and tell the Lord how grateful my wife and I are for our new son." It was Thompson down front. "I can't tell you how much joy this first child has brought into our home. The family is the unit of salvation. A man simply isn't complete until he has a wife and children. It is these relationships that give life its real meaning. I am grateful to the Lord that I know that Nancy and I will have our son and each other all through eternity if we keep the commandments. I know now more than ever that the gospel is true. In the name of Jesus Christ. Amen."

Glen felt the pressure and warmth of Eric's shoulder against his. This morning when he ordained Eric a priest and then shook his hand, it was the first time he had touched Eric in weeks. He had increased his own life insurance twice before Eric was a year old. Now Eric twisted away if even his mother tried to kiss or hug him. And he was getting more sarcastic. Yesterday they'd had another of their little talks about that.

"He's a good boy, Glen," Helen had said, after Eric left the room.

"He doesn't always act like it."

"I guess that we just have to be more patient."

Glen raised his hand, took the mike. On the other side of the chapel, Sylvia Tucker was finishing her testimony. He waited, leg muscles tight, his left hand on the back of the next bench. Eric looked straight ahead.

Swallowing hard, Glen rose above the heads. Faces turned to look up at him, then turned back. He saw the bald heads, blue hair, wigs, hats, white shirts. Speaking into the mike, he told how grateful he was for the neighborhood, the sense of neighborhood, for living in Provo, for the peace they all shared.

"I am grateful," he said, "for the organization of the Church, for all of the good people who help to make the programs work so that we help each other raise our children. My life has taught me that if a man will live the principles of the gospel, he will receive the promised blessings because the gospel works. And he will be able to stand amid all the evil, change, and uncertainty today and give his family a good anchor. It is my testimony that God lives, that Jesus is the Christ, and that Joseph Smith was a prophet of God, as is the president of the Church today. And I want to tell Eric publicly how much his mother and I love him and how proud we are that he is our son and worthy to be ordained a priest. We hope that he will always have a strong testimony of the gospel and keep the commandments, and be worthy to go on a mission. I bear you this testimony in the name of Jesus Christ. Amen."

Glen handed the mike to the waiting Hammond

148

boy and sat down. Eric had leaned forward to rest his forehead on the top of the next bench.

His heart still beating hard, but slowing down, Glen lifted his arm and put it around Helen, pulled her closer to him. She put her hand on his knee. He wanted to start family prayer, to do genealogy, start going to the temple regularly, and start studying the scriptures at least an hour every day.

The Church gave a man a framework for his life, something to believe in, something to hope for, gave him values that made a difference, created emotions. And he wanted to put his arms around Eric and say, "Oh, son, son, do you know of a better way to live? Just tell me." Still flying together, the two hornets bumped along the wall now, didn't light on the windows, flew just above the heads, people leaning away.

Old Brother Hansen rose above the heads to take the traveling mike from the deacon in the other aisle. "I know that God lives, that Jesus is the Christ, that Joseph Smith was a prophet of God, that our prophet today is divinely inspired, and that our Book of Mormon is true. Amen." He was eighty. He still sang in the choir.

Behind Glen somewhere Sister Wilson began to speak. He didn't have to turn. She bore her testimony every fast Sunday and always took at least fifteen minutes.

The sound of a car honking came through the open side doors. The visible front half of the red Torino shone in the sunlight. Eric had washed it again yesterday afternoon before he took it for an hour. They had bought the Torino instead of an Impala because that was what Eric wanted if they couldn't have a sports car. After Eric had driven for a month without an accident or a ticket, he could start dating in the car at night, but he couldn't drag Center Street.

Kids spent hours every night doing nothing but driving up and down Center honking at each other, squealing tires, and flipping fast U-turns. Girls parked their fathers' cars to get in with boys they didn't know and drove off. Groups of boys stood around customized cars as if at altars, and the hippie types, some of them pushing drugs, had their vans.

Sister Wilson was beginning to wind down earlier than usual. "I just wanted to say before I end my testimony how pleased I was to see Eric Miller bless the sacrament this morning. He was one of my Junior Sunday School boys. I watch all of my boys. It is a great testimony to see them grow and develop in the gospel and know that they are worthy to be advanced in the priesthood. We have the finest youth in the world right here in our own ward. Well, I guess I'd better sit down. I've taken too long again, but I am so grateful for all of my blessings. In the name of Jesus Christ. Amen."

"Dear brothers and sisters, I just had to stand up today to tell you how wonderful it is to be home again after being away working all summer in California." It was Cindy, Ted Johnson's youngest girl. "The gospel is just so wonderful and you're all such wonderful people and I appreciate you so much after being away. I know I'm going to cry, but it's just so good to be back home in Provo again where everything is so peaceful and nice. I appreciate my family so much more now and all the things they have done for me. I want to tell them that I love them all so very much."

Eric still sat leaning forward, resting his forehead on top of the next bench. Glen looked up at the clock.

They had twenty minutes left. He reached out and put his hand on Eric's shoulder for a moment, then took it away again. Eric's suit coat shone in the light. His grandmothers had bought him the new tie, shirt, and shoes to go with his new suit, and Bob, Kirsten, and Carie had put their money together to buy him a belt and a matching pair of socks. Long hair, beards, wild clothes, slovenliness, and half-nudity scared Glen, but it was the well-dressed kids on drugs that scared him the most.

Boys from some of the best Church families in Provo turned their brains into sponges, were on drugs for a year before their parents ever found out. They were clean-cut, wore the best clothes, went to their meetings, blessed the sacrament, were boys everybody in the ward expected to go on missions. They had been loved, raised in the Church, been taught right from wrong, to believe in God, had the priesthood, had every comfort a kid could reasonably expect, had a good family, and still they used drugs, as if all those good things meant nothing. Phil and Sue Rogers had mortgaged their home to pay the psychiatrists for Craig. Sue had all but had a nervous breakdown.

"Ah, Dad," Eric said when he spoke to him about drugs, "you don't understand."

"What do you mean, I don't understand?"

"Ah, everybody exaggerates."

"Exaggerates? Do you happen to know what the heroin addiction rate is in this country among adolescents?"

"Ah, good grief."

Over on the right side of the chapel under the windows, Sister Madsen stood up and took the mike from the deacon. David, her oldest son, was a full colonel in the Air Force. Mark was a dentist, and the youngest, Arlo, was an engineer. All three had gone on missions, were married, had good families, and were active in the Church.

A widow for twenty-five years, she was one of those women who kept the Church going. She had worked all her life in the Primary, Junior Sunday School, M.I.A., and Relief Society. Without the women like her, the Church would never make it. Women didn't have to worry about religion; it was natural to them; it was the way they thought about things.

One of the Hansen girls came up the aisle leading her little brother by the hand. The restroom traffic had begun. A few people were turning to look up at the clock. Glen checked his watch, the clock, then glanced at Eric, who still sat bent forward, head resting on the top of the next bench.

But Eric raised up when Jeff White started to speak. Jeff taught the priest quorum. "I bore my testimony just last month when I returned from my mission, brothers and sisters, but I want to bear it again this morning. I know that the power of the Holy Ghost is real. I know the power of prayer and fasting because I I have used that power. I have seen whole families come into the Church and change their lives. I promise any priest here today that if he will go into the mission field and work hard, and have faith, he will receive the promised blessings and testimony. He will learn what love is. I know that the gospel is true. I say these things in the name of Jesus Christ. Amen."

Sylvia Myers stood with the other microphone.

Glen turned to see Eric's face, but he was looking

out through the open door at the Torino. The polished chrome bumper reflected sunlight like a mirror. Glen turned to look straight ahead again. Eric could drive into Wyoming, Idaho, or Nevada on a date now. He could buy liquor, drugs, take a girl to a motel two hundred miles away from Provo. When Glen came out in the morning to drive to the office, Eric still asleep upstairs, the Torino could stand in the driveway dusty in the sunlight, the windshield splattered with dead green insects, the gas tank empty when he turned on the key. For the first month Eric wasn't supposed to drive with more than one of his friends in the car.

Glen looked at Eric, then up at the clock. He closed his eyes and willed Eric to stand up, bear his testimony, do it for his mother's sake, if for no other reason, which he ought to be able to understand.

Maxwell's voice sounded behind Glen, already talking before the deacon could get the mike to him. Glen breathed deep. "My dear brothers and sisters, I feel impressed this morning to rise to my feet and tell you of an experience my good wife and I had while visiting our son and his family in Los Angeles last week. Those of us living in Utah in the safety of the valleys of the Rocky Mountains just don't know how truly blessed we are to be out of Babylon. . . ."

Sister Clinger stood up next and told about a grandson's miraculous recovery from heart surgery and how grateful she was for the power of the priesthood to heal, her voice gradually weakening until she was crying softly, but she went on to finish her testimony, everybody hushed. The lower hornet bumped along the wall, moving toward the open side door, just low enough to hit the top, and then it was gone.

Sister Broadbent bore her testimony. Eric looked straight ahead now. Five minutes. Helen was smiling. After the next testimony, the pause came, ward members turning to look up at the clock, up at Bishop Simmons. The second hornet rose higher, bumped along the top of the middle window again, lit.

Bishop Simmons stood up to the pulpit. "Brothers and sisters, I think that the spirit of the Lord has been here in rich abundance this morning." Glen lifted the song book from the rack. Eric took the other one. Helen's mother was helping Kirsten and Carie with a song book. Sister Monroe, the organist, moved out of the choir seats back to the organ. "I think that we all have been spiritually fed. We will bring our meeting to a close by singing number sixty-four, 'Hope of Israel.' Brother Wayne Spencer will offer the closing prayer." The organ music started, and Sister Lund stood up, lifted her white baton.

Halfway through the first verse Glen began to hear Eric's voice above his own and Helen's. Eric held his song book high so that he could watch Sister Lund directing. Glen lowered his own voice. Eric looked straight ahead, his voice clear, strong. Glen let his own voice gradually drop off, stopped singing, but he didn't turn. Eric's voice was strong, the words familiar to him. Eric raised his eyes from the book to sing the last verse, enjoying the song, feeling it, unmindful of everyone else, but his voice with theirs, singing.

UNDER THE COTTONWOODS

Paul kept both sweaty hands on the steering wheel and breathed through his mouth. Her diaper dirty, Lisa lay just behind him in the back of the station-wagon on the mattress. Valerie was asleep farther back and Richard lay over behind Beth. Richard had stopped crying for Lisa's bottle, but he still whimpered. They had just passed the Lehi turnoff, and from the elevation of the freeway Utah Lake glared to the west like a huge aluminum roof in the afternoon August sun. The air conditioning on the new Buick had gone out just after they left Reno, but now Beth was afraid that if they rolled down the windows another hornet might get in and sting one of the children. He'd had to stop and kill a hornet just before they came to Lehi, and since then the only circulation had been the air vents.

Paul glanced over at Beth. Five months pregnant, she sat sweaty and flushed, silent, one of her church books open on her lap. Counting miscarriages, it was her seventh pregnancy in the nine years they had been married. He had wanted to fly out from San Francisco and rent a car in Salt Lake City, but Beth said that they would need the big new Buick for all of the running around the wedding would involve. His brother Mark, a year home from his mission, was getting married, and Beth's sister Stephanie was the maid of honor. If they had flown out he might have had an extra day on Strawberry Reservoir fishing. It would be nice to fish two days instead of just one. As a boy he had always fished the lower Provo River, until the army engineers gutted it on flood control.

Even while he was in dental school and then later in his orthodontics residency, they had tried to get home on vacation each summer, but it wasn't always a rest. One year they stayed with his parents, the next with Beth's, and it seemed as if they had a family dinner or a canyon picnic every evening, with both families invited, including his and Beth's married brothers and sisters and their children. One night his mother always had the neighbors and family friends over for a buffet on the back lawn, and the mothers of the boys he had known told him about their sons, who were doctors, lawyers, professors, and engineers, told what positions they held in the Church, how many children they had, if they had bought new houses. But the mothers whose sons had not achieved were silent, told him what a fine example he was. One night three mothers told him that.

All his life he had been an example. At first he had to be an example for his younger brothers and sisters, then for the neighborhood boys, for his classmates. In the army he had to be the example of a Mormon for his whole company, never do or say anything that would discredit the Church. His example was supposed to help other servicemen to become interested in the

Church, investigate it, join. And before they would do that they had to find that he was clean, wholesome, spiritual, happy, different from them, had something they didn't have, which they would ask him about. On his mission he had to be an example for his junior companion, for the elders in his zone when he became a zone leader, and finally for all of the elders in the mission when he became assistant to the mission president. When he went to Washington to dental school, he had to be an example too, both he and Beth had to, for all the dental students and their wives. Now in the Palo Alto Ward he had to be an example for all of the Stanford students; he and Beth were what they wanted to become. It was is if being an example were more important than being a person.

He even felt guilty when he took a day of their vacation to go fishing, was away from the family when the vacation was so short. He liked Strawberry best in the late evening when most of the other fishermen had gone home, the boat motors silent, lights on in the fishing camps. Then he fly fished for the big rainbow trout, waded out in the dark cool water with hip boots, used a weighted bubble on his monofilament line to cast his fly seventy or eighty feet out, trolled it back slowly, waited there in the darkness for a big fish to strike, watched the circles where they fed in the moonlight or jumped silver into the air. The Provo River German browns were gold and the Strawberry rainbows rose-silver.

"Richard, be quiet. You're too big for Lisa's bottle."

"He'll be all right, dear," Beth said, "as soon as we get home. He's just tired."

From the freeway Paul watched the whole valley pass. New homes lined the edges of the Orem bench on the left, many of the orchards gone now where he picked fruit as a boy, and new homes lined the roads below the freeway. From Lehi on he had watched for a flock of pigeons but had seen only gulls flying toward the lake. Because the gulls had rescued Brigham Young and the pioneers from the crickets, they were the state bird, protected by state law. As a boy he rode his bike down the county roads trying to spot flocks of pigeons by the flash of their wings in the sun when they wheeled. His flock had all been white. He had traded all over Provo for white pigeons because he liked to see them flying over the neighborhood against the blue sky. At night, his bedroom window open, he lay and listened to the pigeons cooing in their coop on the side of the garage.

But after he was thirteen or fourteen, he couldn't remember being a boy. He had graduated from Provo High School, filled a mission for the Church, been in the army, gotten married, graduated from B.Y.U. and then dental school, finished an orthodontics residency and been in practice one year. He would build a house, a clinic of his own, he and Beth would have three or four more children, and he would probably move up from second counselor to bishop of the Palo Alto Ward, be on the high council, maybe be stake president in ten years. He had done and would do all of those things he was expected to, but his whole life seemed so ordered, predetermined, rushed, tense. At times he felt like a robot, had little sense of controlling his own life, being individual.

He needed memories of his boyhood for balance now, a knowledge that at one time in his life he had been spontaneous, free, full of emotion without obligation, unaware of time, purely physical. But he didn't have that horde of memories he could bring out and look at. In his yearbooks he was a serious-looking, almost fierce boy in a tie and long-sleeved shirt who was a member of the chemistry and mathematics clubs and vice-president of his seminary class. Because he had an after-school job, he hadn't played any varsity sports or been in any school plays. He was never the most preferred boy, a student-body officer, or member of the junior prom committee. He was the student with the third highest grade point average to graduate his year. When he looked at the pictures of all the pretty girls who had been his classmates, he couldn't remember kissing any of them. And among the pictures of the boys he found few that were the faces of friends.

"Paul, hadn't we better stop at the rest area and clean up a little before we get home?" Beth turned to look at him. "I need to change the baby, and I don't want your mother to see us looking like this."

"Okay." They always stopped to clean up before they drove into Provo.

They passed Geneva Steel Plant—two miles of railroad tracks, tanks, towers, smokestacks, blast furnaces, and metal buildings all shimmering in the heat and the thin grey smoke. His mother would come running out to take the children to bathe them and get them ready for supper. Later they would sleep in the clean fresh beds in Jim's room. Jim, his youngest brother, was on a mission in Brazil. Beth's parents would come over as soon as she called them. The house would be gleaming, everything scrubbed, polished, and washed, the refrigerator and freezer full of food, and the lawns like carpet. Every summer his mother spent two or three weeks preparing for their visit, and the order and cleanliness, he knew, were a physical expression of her love. He had spent his life trying to achieve the happiness and perfection his mother wanted for him, and now he was doing it for Beth.

Ahead on the left, running at right angles to the freeway, a line of cottonwood trees marked the Provo River, the biggest clump marking the spot where their swimming hole had been by the railroad bridges. The water had been fifteen feet deep off the big flat boulders they called the ledge. The cottonwoods were like a great green tent, the river making everything cool in spite of the hot Utah desert sun. And they swam, dived, swung out on their rope swing, had water fights, played tag, their brown naked wet bodies flashing in the sun like metal when they left the shade. Each group of boys had a favorite hole, the river a series of holes for six or seven miles from the mouth of the canyon to the lake. No one bothered them except the older boys, who, after they were finished in the fruit orchards, swam in the late afternoons. Tired, he liked to float, close his eyes against the sun, or to lie on the warm ledge and drop pellets of bread to the minnows, watch for trout. But when Provo grew after the War and people started building houses along the river, the army engineers walked their big Caterpillars down the river bed to pile up rock flood-control dikes, tear out all the holes, make a canal out of the river. That had ended the swimming and the fishing.

The "Rest Area" sign came up. Paul flipped on the blinker, lifted his foot off the gas and turned in, stopping in a patch of shade under three cottonwoods that the state road commission had managed to leave standing. The cement walk led to the fountain, three canopied green picnic tables, and the square new restrooms.

"Come on, miserable," he said, and reached back over the seat to pull Richard out by the arm, took one of the blankets and spread it in the shade. Valerie was still asleep by the back window. When he gave Richard Lisa's bottle, he was quiet.

"Oh, honey," Beth said, "he's too old. You'll ruin his training." She knelt on the seat to reach in the back for the diaper bag.

"Anything to keep him quiet for five minutes." Two big Diesels pounded by trailing black exhaust. Across the freeway and along the river the big cotton-woods around the hole, some of them six or seven feet thick and eight feet high, were still standing. The hundred-yard-wide band of willows and trees along both sides of the river was gone except for the big trees. He had been back to stand there on the ledge, which still remained, and look at the channel lined with white glaring rocks. He had been alive there under the trees, full of a kind of freedom, sensation, and pure careless joy he had never known afterward, a sense of being.

He turned. "I'll be back in ten or fifteen minutes, Beth. I'm going to walk over to the river."

"Oh, Paul honey, we haven't got time now for you to go over to that swimming hole of yours. Your mother expects us for supper and we all have to bathe first."

They had stopped to call from Salt Lake City. He looked at his watch. It was four-thirty. "We've got time," and he was already walking. He would hurry. He had told Beth about the swimming hole, and last year driving in on the new freeway he slowed down to point out the trees. He talked about it to friends and even to patients. Paul slid down through the space between the bridge abutment and the chain-link fence and climbed down the high rock dike to where the hornets lit along the trickle of water in the bottom, the only water that came down the channel except during the spring runoff. When he got under the freeway bridges and up on the cut hay field, Beth honked at him. She stood pointing at her watch. He waved, walked across the field and into the trees, where it was cooler. He stopped to look up into the high limbs, breathe the cottonwood smell, then walked through the trees out onto the shaded ledge. With the water gone the real coolness was gone too, along with all the frogs, minnows, and trout.

The hole had been about half the size of a tennis court, and smooth, just enough water flowing in and out to keep it fresh and cool. The first thing that he always did once he got his clothes pulled off was to run and dive as far out as he could off the ledge, cut down, down, down, into the cool clear water, then shoot up out of it again, the water giving him sensation all over. He ran and dived many times, then finally stayed under, glided smooth and clean, pushing with his arms, following minnows. When he swung out on the rope swing, the air cooled his wet naked body, and when he let go, dropped, the sensation went up through to his skull. Later, spread-eagled on the ledge with the other boys, he felt his body full of the sensation of heat.

He liked to fish alone. He pulled on his Levis, the copper rivets burning his skin, put on his gym shoes, took his pole and walked up through the trees. He waded in the river, rolled his worm through the

162

shaded holes and pockets, caught chubs, suckers. Tap, tap, tap, the trout bit, then hooked, fought, went deep, made sudden rushes, the pole an extension of his arm, bringing the feeling into his body, connecting him and the trout. Tired, the trout rose out of the deep water, flashed gold, the rushes shorter, and he pulled it up onto the rocks, held it in both hands to smash its head, cleaned it, threw the entrails to the gulls. Fresh from the water the German browns were beautiful, gold with red, black, and orange dots like jewels, but the beauty faded. When he took fish home his father told him about the big ones he had caught on the river as a boy.

Reaching down, Paul picked up one of the warm, water-smooth rocks, held it for a moment then lobbed it out into the channel. A gull flew past him low going upstream, turning its head from side to side looking for something to eat. He was eight when he first saw the gold monument to the gulls on Temple Square in Salt Lake City.

His father convinced his mother that it was safe for him to swim in the river, but before he could go he had to practice the piano and finish his work. He weeded, hoed, and irrigated the garden, mowed, trimmed, raked, and watered the lawn, weeded the front flower beds, washed the house windows on the outside, washed the car for Sunday. The checks on his mother's daily list showed that he had worked hard, been a good example for his younger brothers and sisters. And when he began to do jobs for his grandmother's friends, who paid him, his mother helped him keep an account of his money so that he could pay his tithing. Most of his money he saved for his mission and college, although he could spend some.

His mother said, "Everything you do is a reflection of yourself, Paul. People know you by what you do." He believed this, saw that it was true, and out of pride, love for his mother and father, he wanted to do everything right, fulfill their high opinion of him, reward their hard work and struggle, be an example. The polished windows, trimmed neat lawns, weedless garden became a mirror of himself, like his clothes, speech, and Sunday School attendance, his Boy Scout badges. When he pulled weeds it was as if he pulled them out of his own flesh, and he was impatient for them to dry so that he could burn them. Work was moral. Thus he became fierce about right and wrong younger than most boys, sought the perfection he was taught was possible, believed he too would become a god.

Work took him away from the river the summer before the army engineers destroyed it. He didn't have time any more for play, or if he did it was only in the evenings or when the Orem farmers didn't have cherries, apricots, peaches, pears, or apples to be picked, because at fourteen he was old enough to work in the orchards, fill the baskets with fruit. Sweaty, his mouth dry with dust from the trees, he broke off stems until the ends of his fingers became numb. He worked both hands at a time, kept a steady stream of fruit going into the canvas bag, felt the growing weight against his stomach and loins, tried to pick more than the other boys. In his mind he added up how much money he was making at five cents a bushel, knew how much it was possible to make in an hour. He stopped only to eat lunch or, standing on a high ladder, to watch the farmer's flock of pigeons wheeling over the orchard. When he quit work each afternoon, he looked down the row of trees to see the sixty or seventy baskets of peaches, pears, or apples he had picked. He didn't like the farmer to haul any of his baskets off before the end of the day. He was always anxious to get home to tell his mother how much he had picked.

"You'll make a fine dentist, son," she often said, encouraged him. She wanted him to have a better life than his father had working for the Union Pacific Railroad in the shops. All the mothers in the neighborhood were ambitious for their sons, talked of their going on to college, graduating, going to medical school, dental school, law school, graduate school, set them to work early to earn their way if their fathers couldn't afford the educations their mothers wanted for them. And in this way they were already in competition with each other at fourteen and fifteen, although they didn't know that then.

He became frantic about time. He had a calendar in his room, a clock, wore a watch, became aware of seconds, minutes, hours, days, weeks, months. The work had to be done well, but it had also to be accomplished in a given time. There was so much to do, so little time to do it in—practice the piano, go to school, work, study, be active in the Church. He had to be able to look back on a day and see what he had done with his twenty-four hours, how he had used them. Money earned and things accomplished, Boy Scout and priesthood awards and badges won became a way of measuring time. And he had a time chart on his wall, put little checks in the squares, made a new chart each month, saved the old charts in a pile because they showed what he had done, were another way to measure time. Two years on a mission, six months in the army, four years in college, four in

dental school, two in his residency, one in practice—
his life had become too much an exercise in the proper
use of time.

Paul listened. Behind him a steady pattern of honking came through the trees from the freeway. It was
Beth. He looked at his watch. He should go. Another
gull flew up the channel. Gulls worked. They
searched the lake shore and the river banks for dead
fish, fed on insects in the freshly plowed ground,
dropped onto the streets of Provo to pick up fallen ice
cream cones, parts of sandwiches, fruit, patrolled
Strawberry Reservoir to consume the red entrails of
cleaned fish. Gulls were heavy slow birds, never
seemed to be flying, but walking, not like his pigeons.
Evenings he climbed up the telephone pole at the back
of their yard so that he could watch his white pigeons
flying over the houses and trees. When he fed them
from his hand, they circled the back yard, fluttered
down to him, their white wings flashing in the
twilight.

Something else had happened to him here that
summer he was fourteen which helped to stop his
boyhood. He became aware of his body and through it
his inner self. His body had always been for sensing
water, sun and air, and all of his responses were spontaneous, not observed. But lying on the ledge in the
sun the days he wasn't picking fruit, he began to
watch his body. He touched his arms, legs, chest, ran
the flat of his hand over his new muscles, became
aware finally that he was male. And at times his whole
being seemed focused in his loins. Arms wrapped
around his legs, he pulled tight, chin resting on his
knees, watched the water, waited for a voice to explain
to him the chemistry of his pounding blood.

The boy's folklore of sex didn't help him understand puberty because for him the body was sacred, an instrument for the purposes of God and not his own, to provide temples for the spirits waiting to come to earth to be reared in Mormon homes. He had to be clean, pure; sexual sin was next in evil to the shedding of innocent blood. Sex wasn't freedom, delight, or interest, but already obligation, a topic he couldn't talk about with other boys because he had to be an example, be perfect. He turned inward on himself to watch his every emotion, which led him to discover hate, lust, vanity, jealousy, and rage, that goodness was inside, not outside. He became preoccupied with his own guilt. The Sunday School lessons, priesthood lessons, Boy Scout oath and law, all the things his mother taught him, all the commandments that hung over him like a net, fell, and he grew silent, stabbed his sins alone.

"What's the matter, Paul?" his father asked him one Sunday that summer after dinner. "Something wrong?"

"Yes, don't you feel well, Paul?" his mother said and reached over to put her hand on his forehead.

His father took him swimming one evening after that. "I thought that we might go down to that swimming hole of yours, Paul. You've been working hard out in the peaches." His father's naked body was pale in the darkness, his stomach soft, his shoulders round and stooped. After his father was in the water, Paul took off his shorts and dove in from the ledge. "This is great, son. We should do it more often." His father laughed, shouted, splashed, got up on the ledge once to run and dive in, all the time telling him how much fun he had had on the river as a boy. Once in the darkness their bodies touched. "Sorry, son." But then under the cottonwoods in the dark water shaded from the moon, his father became silent, the only sounds the crickets and frogs, the splash of a heavy fish in the next hole. His father was silent when they got out to dry themselves with towels. They stopped at Cook's Ice Cream for malts on the way home. "Well, son, would you like another one?"

"No thanks, Dad."

"You're welcome to it."

He shook his head. They sat silent in the booth for a moment, then his father paid and they left, and his father put his hand on his shoulder as they walked to the car.

He wanted to talk to his father, ask him many questions, hear answers, but he couldn't. He couldn't admit to what he felt, to his emotions, drives, new appetites, thought that he might hurt his father's high opinion of him, sadden his father. He wanted to do and be all of those things his parents expected of him; he wanted the perfection, the godhood his mother talked about; he would sacrifice anything for her belief in that, even himself. So he couldn't talk to his father, use his father's understanding instead of his own. He couldn't let his father protect his boyhood for him, shield him for another three or four years, help him avoid the developing fierceness about his own life.

Reaching down, Paul picked up a dry branch, began to break off small pieces and flip them into the channel. He had become lonely. It was easier not to have too many friends, easier to believe in his own perfection that way. He didn't really talk to his classmates, fellows in the army, missionary companions, let them be part of him, touch him. Even with

Beth now, as much as he loved her, it was hard to talk, to tell her what was inside, what he really felt, and for the same reasons. He didn't want to hurt her or lessen her opinion of him, suggest that perhaps he had not been or was not all that she had thought, hoped, imagined. He tried very hard to be the kind of person she wanted him to be, or the kind he thought she wanted him to be. At times he had the feeling that he was an actor performing a role in a play.

After that one night his father never swam with him again, but Paul rode his bicycle down alone in the evenings that summer to fish. He fished in the darkness, had learned to fly fish, cast the big wet fly where the German brown trout came up in the shallows to feed on minnows. He bought a dip net so that he could hold the trout in the water, shine his flashlight down to see them gold and jeweled before he killed and cleaned them to take home. His mother wrapped them in wax paper and they faded white before she fried them. When he swam at night he swam quietly, head up, or floated, listened, watched the stars through the openings in the cottonwoods. He held onto the swing, the arches slowly growing shorter until the swing stopped, his feet touching the water, then let go, slipped down into the water, stayed under as long as he could. He didn't take a towel, stood to let the night breeze dry his body.

Out of his desire for purity, he became preoccupied with being physically clean. He showered twice a day, polished his shoes every time he left the house, combed his hair at every mirror and window, carried a toothbrush in his briefcase, changed his shirts twice a day, liked to wear fresh ironed shirts. So in this way he lost all delight in his body. He distrusted it, became uneasy because of what he now felt, and so after fourteen he had no memory of his body being wonderful. If he hadn't had to work after school, if he'd had time for football, basketball, wrestling, sensing his body hot, sweaty, breathless, if he'd known that he was like other boys, it would have been better. He didn't follow professional or college sports now, but when he had a chance he went to the Palo Alto High School games and meets, tried to imagine himself passing, catching the ball, shooting baskets, running, swimming, see himself, live it all vicariously. He wanted to find his body, take back the responsibility for his own life so that he could begin to love out of himself.

Beth was honking again. Paul flipped the last piece of the branch into the channel, turned, and walked back through the trees and out into the sun, stopping in the hay stubble to pull the cheat grass from his socks. Beth sat in the Buick with the front doors open when he got back to the rest area. Lisa had her bottle, Richard played with a string of plastic blocks on the mattress, and Valerie lay on her stomach coloring. Beth put her book down, got out and walked to the fountain and dampened a clean diaper. "You look hot, darling," she said and handed it to him. He wiped off his sweaty face, neck, and hands. Beth had emptied the litter bag, wiped the fingerprints off the inside of the windows, straightened up the back of the stationwagon, put on new makeup and combed her hair. "Your shoes are dusty." He wiped them off and she took the diaper back. He put on the clean shirt she had gotten out for him, tipping the sideview mirror back to comb his hair.

"Your mother will be wondering where we are.

She will think that we had an accident."

"Yes, I guess she will. I'm sorry that I took so long, dear."

He tightened his seat belt, pulled out to the freeway, then nosed into the heavy late-afternoon traffic. They crossed the river, and the Provo exit sign came up. Going up on the off ramp he saw the tops of trees and houses, felt the old surge of joy he always felt at coming home, remembered how he had felt when he returned from his mission and the army, how fiercely he loved home. They came off the loop and drove up Center Street past all of the new service stations built for the freeway traffic and then past Pioneer Park, stopping at the semaphore on Fifth West. Richard climbed over into the front seat. "Grandmaw," he said, "Grandmaw."

Paul turned right on Third West, then left on Second South. Except that the old Provo High School building had been torn down, the neighborhood hadn't changed; all of the new houses and construction were in the northeast part of town. The corner telephone pole had always been the goal for their games of grey wolf and kick the can. "There's Mark sitting on the porch with your mother and father. I wonder where Darlene is?" Beth started to wave.

"She's probably got plenty to do if they're getting married Wednesday, honey," he said.

His mother, father, and Mark started down the steps waving as he turned into the driveway.

After the welcome was over and his mother and Beth had taken the children into the house to bathe them and get them ready for supper and bed, he, Mark, and his father unloaded the Buick. Later, standing on the front porch alone with Mark, he asked him if he wanted to go fishing up on Strawberry one evening before he got married. "Sure," Mark said, "I've been planning on it just like every summer and so has Dad."

"Good." He still had his old spinning outfit, although he had bought new hip boots. In the darkness he would stand in the thigh-deep cool water, cast out into the lake, slowly troll the fly in, every second expecting a strike, see the beautiful silver rainbow trout leap shining in the moonlight. Mark and his father would kill the trout they caught, clean them, leave the entrails on the shore for the patrolling gulls the next morning. But he wouldn't. After he had fought a trout, felt the movement and pull, the heavy pulse coming up through the line and rod into his hand and arm, seen it in front of him in the water, he would free it. He would hold the rainbow in the net to see it shining rose-silver, pull the hook from the lip, then release it, see the trout hover then flash back into the deep water, vanish.

INDIAN HILLS

Reed turned off his car lights and then leaned forward to press his forehead against the steering wheel. Clark and he had played basketball and tennis for Provo High, gone on their missions the same month, graduated from B.Y.U. together, and had for six years now lived in the same Indian Hills ward. Because Camille had called him right after she called Dr. Peters, Reed had arrived while they were still working for a heartbeat, Clark lying on the garage floor.

Reed had covered Clark with the blanket and folded it again when the Berg Mortuary people spread the white sheet over him. And all the time Reed kept thinking that Clark was a doctor and should have had better sense than to let himself have a heart attack or stroke or whatever it was that killed him. He should have stayed in shape.

Reed had hugged Camille and said fiercely, "He's still yours. You and the boys will all be together again in the next life. Dying isn't really the end of anything is it?" Her tears had wet through his sport shirt and garments, and he could not describe the sound she made. He had put his arm around each of Clark's three boys and told them that their dad was alive in heaven.

Reed raised his head from the steering wheel when Marilyn turned on the carport light and opened the side door. He got out of the car. He put his arms around her. She was seven months pregnant. "Oh, Reed, it's so terrible. How is Camille?"

"Bad. Dr. Peters gave her a shot. Clark's folks are there now and Camille's are flying in from Denver tomorrow morning. The bishop was over and they had a prayer for Camille and the boys. The house is full of neighbors."

"Didn't she want a blessing?"

"No, just a prayer for the whole family."

"Oh, Reed, I can't think of Clark dead. You're the same age." He held her tighter. "Maybe I should have gone with you."

"Not in your condition. You can go over when things have calmed down a little." He was glad she didn't cry; he'd had enough of crying for one night. He kissed her again. "Come on, let's go in. The kids all asleep?"

"Yes, hours ago. Even Brad, though he wanted to stay up until you got home. You must be exhausted."

"A little."

The house, as if resting, was all clean and ready for Sunday, but it was still warm. The swamp cooler wasn't working again. Marilyn had the patio doors open to pick up any breeze. They sat down on the sofa. "Oh brother," he said and lay back.

"Why don't you take off your shoes, honey?"

He pulled off his shoes and socks and spread his toes wide on the carpet. The sofa faced the patio and he looked out through the screen and above the roofs

174

to the black silhouette of mountains against the east night sky. Their friends who had view lots saw west across the whole valley. Clark had built on a knoll that gave a view on every side.

"It seems such a terrible waste," Marilyn said. "Clark was a good doctor, Camille is beautiful, and they have those three fine boys. The whole family was active in the Church. Clark had absolutely everything a man could want. Maybe the Lord needed him."

Reed almost said, "Who really knows what the Lord needs?" He took her hand. Clark wasn't that prepared to die. After the first absolute numbness, all Reed had felt was anger because Clark had been such a fool. He had worked night and day since he had finished his residency and started to practice. In eight years he had bought a home, half a dozen different new cars, a cabin at Sundance, a four-wheel drive truck with a camper, a boat, and he had become a partner in his own clinic. Reed knew that with his doctorate and an associate professorship at B.Y.U., he probably made a third or maybe a fourth of what Clark did . . . had.

Marilyn's hand was warm. Clark's would be the sixth funeral for them in the five months since he had come home from the hospital after his kidney infection —two faculty members had died, Aunt Nelly (they needed the whole family in one big fenced-in plot), Brother Cluff from his old neighborhood, and a freshman. People were dying by the thousands of cholera epidemics in India and Pakistan, and thousands died daily in the world of starvation or in the little wars. And there were the airliner crashes, skyscraper fires, mine disasters, California multi-car freeway accidents, and the bomb explosions.

He was becoming almost nervous about picking up the *Herald* or the *Tribune* or turning on the TV for the 6 o'clock news. In their Sunday School class somebody was always saying that the last days were here and that every family should have its year's supply of food, fuel, and clothing put away.

Clark shouldn't be dead. They had been best friends all through high school. People said that they looked enough alike to be brothers. But other friends their age had heart problems, high blood pressure, emphysema, cancer now, so were becoming sick with the diseases that would kill them eventually.

His kidney infection had knocked him out for a month, the pain bad at times and the weakness almost absolute. The day Doctor Hayes talked of his right kidney's maybe giving out, assuring him all the time that one kidney was enough, he had another blessing. That night before the sleeping tablets finally put him out, he lay trying to feel his love for the Lord and his belief in eternal life. It had to be a feeling, one at least as strong as the fear. He wanted to escape time, not have any emotion for time. He kept reaching up to feel the pulse in his throat with his fingers.

When he drove up Tenth East he saw the vaults stacked behind the Beezley Monument Company, rows of them, in adult and child sizes. Clark's vault had been made for months, maybe even a year.

"How's the infant?"

"Oh, fine. He's been very quiet all day."

Marilyn put her right hand on her stomach. The light from the floor lamp behind the sofa led out through the screen and across the patio to the edge of the darker lawn. All his life he had been taught that the family was the unit of exaltation. You didn't get far in the celestial kingdom alone.

"Did Brad get the lawn finished, honey?"

"Yes. He even raked it. He was upset about Clark, so I was glad that he had something to do. He wanted to stay up and watch the late movie until you got home."

"Did he wash off the driveway?"

"Yes."

When Reed had driven in, Ted Willard still stood watching his sprinkling system plume in the moonlight as he kept that much of the world green. (Thursday Ted had him down in his basement again to show him some new shelves he had built to hold his year's supply of canned goods.) Walking past the cut lawns, hosed-off driveways, and washed cars was part of going to church on Sunday morning.

Marilyn took her hand from his and put her hand on his knee. "How did the boys take it?"

"Mark found him."

"Oh, how terrible."

"Doctor Peters gave all three of the boys shots too."

"Well at least they'll get some sleep tonight."

"I suppose."

Reed half turned his head to glance down the hall toward Brad's and the girls' rooms. He wanted to say, "But children need to remember the night their father dies. How do they deal with it if they lay drugged and don't know how they felt?" A father deserved that much.

He kept seeing Clark when they were playing basketball and tennis and running the mile. Their bodies hard, seeming almost to reflect light, they had not even imagined the possibility of their own deaths, or even their fathers' deaths. Clark always liked to get a towel fight started in the showers.

Lying on the cement garage floor, Clark had reminded him of a dead rabbit or deer. Clark had still hunted as much as ever, used his four-wheel drive truck a lot for that, but Reed had finally quit two years ago. His last season he had run across the partially decomposed body of a big four-point buck he had wounded the year before and trailed by the blood into some ledges but hadn't been able to find, and that had ended it for him. Deer hunting was bad because a buck was a large animal. He was glad that Brad didn't want to hunt.

Marilyn lifted her hand from his knee to take his right hand in both of hers. She pressed it to her cheek, and he leaned over and kissed her above the ear, her soft body touching him. "I guess you'd like something to eat wouldn't you?"

"I'm not very hungry, but I guess I should have something."

"How about a bacon and tomato sandwich and hot chocolate, or do you want something cold to drink?"

"No, that's fine. I'd like something hot to drink." (He and Clark used to wash their hamburgers down with long swallows of Pepsi-Cola that burned their throats. Snappy's made the best hamburgers.)

Marilyn squeezed his hand and stood up. "Several people called while you were away. Nobody will believe that Clark is gone." She walked across the living room and into the kitchen, and turned on the light.

Brad had come in from cutting the lawn and was in the kitchen drinking a glass of orange juice when Camille had shouted over the phone, "He's dead! He's dead! Clark's dead!"

"What's wrong, Dad?" Brad had said after he'd hung up the phone. "You look kind of funny."

He had wanted to say, "Dr. Nielsen is very sick, son," but Camille was a registered nurse. "Dr. Nielsen just died, son."

"Gee, he taught me in Sunday School."

"Yes." And then, inexplicably, they had shaken hands.

Sitting there, Reed picked up the morning *Tribune* from the coffee table and unfolded it. The front page was the flareups in Indochina and the Middle East again (someone had told him that there were forty-one wars going on all over the world). He refolded the paper and laid it back down. Tomorrow the *Tribune* would list obituaries for the whole state, the section running to four or five columns. He had begun to see pictures he had last seen in one of his college yearbooks, the pictures small, grey, and out of date. Clark's obituary wouldn't be in until Monday.

Reed looked at his watch. It was too late to phone his mother and tell her about Clark. She got the Provo *Herald* in the evening and *Tribune* in the morning. She phoned him at his office to tell him as soon as she read or heard that some friend, neighbor, or relative had died. A lot of people had died in the old neighborhood in the last ten years, the old houses divided up into apartments for married B.Y.U. students. His mother talked of the dead as if they were still alive.

The houses, sidewalks, and trees in the old neighborhood hadn't changed much, just the people. He wished that Marilyn's father wasn't dead and that her mother and sister lived in Provo. He wished that his three sisters lived in Provo. He needed more uncles and aunts, he needed his grandparents alive. (His

179

father's parents had stayed in England; only his mother's parents had immigrated after they joined the Church.) A big family changed the way a person looked at time.

Death was how a person looked at time. Reed stood up from the sofa. Only Christ had promised immortality. At least he couldn't think of anybody else who had. He saw the bookcase, walked over to it and took down his missionary triple combination and Bible (they were for Brad). He moved over to the lamp and opened the Bible to Matthew and read the marked passages. He had taught the gospel of Christ on his mission. After twenty years his testimony should be like heat and light in his body. Faith was supposed to become knowledge, fact.

"Honey, I'll be ready in a minute."

Marilyn stood in the kitchen doorway. "Okay." Reed put the books on the lamp table and walked over to the screen door. There was still no breeze, but the air was cooler on his naked feet.

The east mountains rose straight up, seemed almost ready to tip down on them all. A view lot would have cost them another three or four thousand at least. Marilyn liked to see out over the valley, see the city lights in the evening, see the twenty-five miles of Utah Lake glittering under the moon. Reed pressed his forehead against the cool aluminum frame and closed his eyes.

He had read in the *Herald* that the lake was higher this year again, the sloughs spreading out farther toward Provo. Every time a big earthquake hit Turkey or Peru, some idiot TV commentator in Salt Lake cornered a University of Utah geologist for comments about the possibility of a major earthquake on the

Wasatch fault. The commentator always gave the same facts: eighty-five percent of the state's population lived in the major valleys along the fault; all of the major canyons feeding into those valleys had dams, some of the reservoirs five miles long and a hundred feet deep. Prehistoric Lake Bonneville had filled the valleys once. Everybody wanted a view lot above the valley floor. The fault ran along the top benches and in some places through Indian Hills.

The sound of the doorbell opened Reed's eyes and pulled his forehead away from the cool aluminum. "I'll get it, honey."

It was Byron Wilson. Reed pushed open the storm door.

"No, Reed, I won't come in. I'm sorry, I know it's past eleven, but we saw your light. We just got back and heard about Clark Nielsen. We just can't believe it. I know you and he were lifelong friends . . ."

"It's hard to believe."

"Why would the Lord take him away from his family now? You just can't believe it."

"No, you can't."

"Well, I won't keep you, Reed. I don't suppose there's anything we can do to help tonight, except pray I guess."

"I guess that's about all."

"Well, it's a wonderful thing that we have testimonies of the gospel at a time like this." They shook hands. "Good night, Reed."

"Good night, Byron."

Reed let the storm door close and watched Byron cross the street. He was in the French Department; half the neighborhood was on the faculty or in the administration. Teaching university students helped to keep a man believing that all the world was young. Death was always by accident in Indian Hills. They needed old people (four families on their block had new babies and all the new houses were either blond or white brick).

Some Provo men had generations in the Church, had old family houses scattered all through Provo, pioneer houses even. And they had family houses and cemeteries in the Midwest, the East, and then England or Europe. A man needed to go back to the Romans, Greeks, Hebrews, connect onto Bible genealogy, go back to Adam.

Byron vanished behind his storm door, and Reed looked out between the Hafen's and Thompson's to the valley lights and Utah Lake under the moon. If he built a tower in the backyard, he and Marilyn could look out over the valley too. As a boy he had climbed telephone poles, high trees, silos, and mountains so that he could see. The earth was supposed to become the celestial kingdom.

Reed reached down and locked the storm door. Every year the valley lights spread farther. A lot of young families were moving in from the West Coast and the East, taking a cut in salary to live in Utah Valley (preferably Provo). The big thing was to be active in the Church, be close to the temple and B.Y.U., and raise your kids away from the drugs, crime, immorality, and race problems. The Church told the members to stay out in the stakes, for the stakes were Zion too, if there was righteousness, but still people came, as if safety were a place. Perfection was safety.

As late as it was, quite a few cars still moved along the freeway, the lights disappearing finally into the darkness down toward Spanish Fork and Payson. He stood there. "Not Clark," he said quietly. Thousands of people in Provo were older than he and Clark. (They both had birthdays the same month.)

Of the five deaths before Clark's, his Aunt Nelly's had bothered him the most. Even seeing her in the casket, he could only imagine her alive. His grandparents' generation was all gone, so now his parents' generation was on the line. After that it would be his generation. (The last year or two he saw the Beezley Monument vault trucks everywhere he went—coming down the canyon, out in Sanpete Valley, on the freeway, even out in the Uintah Basin. He had begun to expect to see them. Sometimes they had a vault, sometimes not, the delivery already made.)

The foyer tile floor was cool under his feet. Turning, Reed walked back into the front room and sat down again on the sofa. Marilyn came in from the kitchen and put two placemats on the coffee table. "I thought that it would be cooler here than in the kitchen. Who was that at the door?"

"Byron. He wanted to know if there was anything he could do."

"The Dixons wanted to get everybody together for a neighborhood prayer, but they thought that the hearse was an ambulance. People just won't be able to believe it. Clark had absolutely everything to live for. I guess there's just a lot we won't understand until we get to the next life."

Reed reached out, took Marilyn's hand, pressed it to the side of his face. Marilyn smoothed down his hair. "By the way, honey, Brad got a call from the *Herald* today to say that they had a route for him."

"Good."

"Well, I'd better get the hot chocolate before it boils over."

Brad's name had been on both the *Trib* and *Herald* lists for over a year, and he had substituted on two different routes. Reed was glad it was a *Herald* route. He'd had a *Herald* route all through high school. He looked down at his feet. He had delivered to the Berg Mortuary. On winter evenings, the crows, come up from the fields, cawed in the trees above him. After the duck season was over, he and Clark went down into the fields to shoot crows. The best spot was behind Kuhni's by-products plant, where the crows came to feed on the twenty-foot-high pile of bones. (He had toured a mortuary once on a high-school field trip to Salt Lake; the stainless steel tables had drains.)

Clark was the best shot. He was good at everything, his body trim and hard, absolutely coordinated. Five thousand people had cheered them in the state basketball finals their senior year, but most of it had been for Clark. He set up all the plays and made the most points; he always had everything under control.

"You and Clark have been friends all of your lives," Marilyn said when she set the tray down in front of him.

"Since the fifth grade."

"The whole thing is terrible."

He was just stirring his hot chocolate when the phone rang. "I'll get it," he said. He brought the phone over to the coffee table.

As he talked he watched the steam rising from the cups, then put the receiver back in the cradle. "Ray saw our lights. He wanted to know if there was anything he could do."

"Everybody will want to help."

184

"There's not much to do."

"I thought that I would get up early and go over and cook breakfast for Camille and the boys, but the house will be full of relatives. I'll wait a few days. She'll need more help then."

"That makes sense, honey."

"Did Ray get his coal?"

"Yes. He told me yesterday they got it." Ray had built a shed for a year's supply of coal. He had bought a new coal-burning stove and stored it in his garage.

Reed drank the hot sweet chocolate. For a week, maybe two, the neighborhood men would cut Clark's lawns, wash his cars; and the women, glad for the opportunity to show charity, would send food, each pyrex dish identified with a name on a piece of masking tape. Perhaps Camille wouldn't be able to go into the garage of her new house. Now people sold houses in which there had been too much grief. (The Prophet Joseph Smith had seen the Father and the Son; other people in the Book of Mormon and the Bible had seen them, and particularly the Son.) His mother and father had lived in the same house since they were married. He liked to be in the old house.

He took another drink of the hot chocolate.

Since his father's retirement, his parents worked in the Provo Temple three days a week. All of the workers were old. When he picked up his mother at the Genealogical Library in Salt Lake, most of the researchers were old. They all wanted to trace every line back to Adam, so have that vision of eternal family. "You'll get the spirit of genealogy when you're older, son," his mother kept telling him. "It's natural." During the millennium there would be thousands of temples to do the endowments for the dead.

185

Reed put his cup back on the saucer. Just above his knees his garments made a ridge under his thin summer pants. At times now he had a frenzy to keep all of the commandments, as if that was the only important thing left to do. And he had moments of terror when he thought how old he was. He needed to use every minute of his life to be righteous. (He wanted to spend at least a half an hour a day reading the scriptures.) Everybody was supposed to want the highest degree of the celestial kingdom so that they could be with their families and with God. He wasn't anybody without Marilyn and the kids. Every day the appointment calendar on his desk grew imperceptibly thicker on the left side. He tried to imagine an appointment calendar for his whole life so far and how thick it would be on the left side.

"You seem awfully quiet, honey. Thinking?"

"A little." He reached over to touch her and then picked up his sandwich. "That's good hot chocolate."

"Will Camille ask you to be one of the speakers?"

"She might; maybe she'll want me to be a pallbearer."

"Sometimes I think that a funeral should just be soft violin music and flowers from people's gardens, and that nobody should say any words."

She turned her head to look up at the black silhouetted mountains.

He held the hot cup in both hands. Mourners didn't like facts. He would have to ignore Clark's closed coffin, the concrete vault, the piled grave dirt covered with a robe of artificial grass. If he spoke, he would be expected to read the important resurrection scriptures, assign Clark to the celestial kingdom, exalt him, make him a potential god who created and peopled worlds of his own, bear his testimony to that.

And he could not tell Clark's mourners that two weeks ago Bob Wiest, his optometrist, had said, "Reed, you have middle-aged eyes. You'll need bifocals next time." He tested his eyes constantly now on distant signs and small print close up, and he tried to remember what he had been able to read last year. His teeth were more sensitive to hot and cold and to sweet foods. He was still losing hair.

When the kidney infection was bad, he kept sinking in grey water, too weak to lift his hands or speak to Marilyn, sank into the darkness, rose again slowly, looked around like a seal surfacing. He kept seeing the pictures that thirty-five years earlier his Junior Sunday School teacher had held up to tell stories about Christ healing the leper, raising Lazarus, answering Pilate, carrying his cross, holding out his hands to Thomas.

Every neighborhood needed someone to have been called back from the dead. The bishop needed to bless the man and bring him back, and then they both needed to testify to what had happened. And it shouldn't seem unnatural. It didn't have to happen often, maybe once out of every thousand deaths. People should accept things like that. Some days he sat in his office thinking about all the people he knew in the Provo Cemetery. (Each family needed a plot with a wrought-iron fence around it.) A person should be able to talk to somebody who had been called back and ask him what it was like.

He jogged daily around the Smith Fieldhouse indoor track with the other faculty members to slow down his heart so that it wouldn't wear out so fast, checking his heartbeat before and after against his watch. Professor Bolls, emeritus, seventy-five or eighty now, jogged, his white flesh jiggling, the bones pushing through. The afternoons the shower was crowded (he took Brad, and the other faculty members had their sons, some only four or five years old) he saw all the stages of man's flesh.

This year for the first time Dr. Stone had suggested an electrocardiogram; his mother had warned him about getting too tired shoveling snow. He had that beginning awareness of heart, lungs, kidneys, and liver wearing out, cholesterol beginning to clog the arteries. And there was biological warfare, world pollution, world starvation, atomic warfare, depletion of all resources. (Located across from the cemetery, the Beezley Monument Company had rows of sample headstones on their front lawn. When he drove by in the evening, down the driveway he saw the parked vault trucks.) He set the cup back on the saucer.

"We should have had a breeze before now," Marilyn said.

"Yes."

He put his arm through hers, and she leaned against him. Toward the end of a pregnancy she always needed to be touched and held more, their bodies meaning less alone. The new baby would have their blood, flesh, and bones again, look like them, their bodies recast again. They and the kids were something whole and beyond themselves, a unity. He reached up to touch Marilyn's beautiful hair. He needed to know all of the scriptures, to be more than only good. All meaning had to be religious, finally.

"Maybe I should have let Brad stay up. He wanted to ask you something. But the movie was one of those horror things again."

The telephone rang.

"Oh, good heavens," Marilyn said. "I wonder who that could be. It's almost twelve o'clock."

Reed picked up the phone. "Reed, this is Keith Jensen. We saw your light or I wouldn't have called. I guess you heard about Clark Nielsen?"

"Yes."

"We just can't believe it. Ruth has been crying ever since we got back and heard about it. He delivered Melissa and Cindy."

"I remember." He spoke to Keith for a few minutes and then hung up.

"Keith Jensen?" Marilyn said.

"Yes. They just got back from Salt Lake."

"Clark was Ruth's doctor."

"Yes, that's what he said."

"Poor Camille. I wonder if she'll go back into nursing."

"Doctors carry big insurance policies."

Marilyn took the tray back into the kitchen. Reed stood up and walked to the screen. At the backs of the houses all the bedroom lights were out. In each house the little drama connected with the news of Clark's sudden death must take place, with its demand for details, proof. Because Clark had been a doctor, his picture in the *Herald* would be larger than the usual one-inch square. Tomorrow in church, ward members would ask each other about Clark. Those who said the prayers would pray for Camille and the boys, and themselves.

Clark had lain on his side in his air-conditioned garage (he had a shop in the garage) staring into the mirror of the Buick hub cap. Reed had backed the

Buick out so that the Berg Mortuary people could bring in their cart. When Richard and the other two boys came out to watch, one of the neighbors had hurried them back into the house. Doctor Peters wouldn't be able to give them a shot every day.

Reading the *Herald* obituaries one evening in the hospital (a patient had died across the hall the day before), he had suddenly realized that he had lived long enough for most of his own obituary to be written. The number of his survivors and the day, place, and cause of his death were the only essential unknown facts of his life. His obituary picture could already have been taken. He needed a birthday picture of himself for every year so that he could see how he had changed. He wanted sometimes to carry all three of his high school yearbooks to his classes and prove to his students that they weren't the only people in the world who had ever been young.

"Dad."

Reed turned from the patio screen. Brad in his blue pajamas stood at the end of the sofa. "Son, what are you doing up? I thought you were asleep hours ago."

"I can't sleep, Dad. I keep thinking about Dr. Nielsen."

"Everything will be all right, son."

"But when I was out doing the lawn this afternoon, he drove by. He honked at me and waved."

"Oh . . ." Then Reed walked over to Brad, put his arm around his shoulder and pulled Brad tight against him. "You believe you'll see Dr. Nielsen again don't you, son? I mean your mother and I have taught you that, and you've learned it in all your Sunday School and priesthood classes haven't you? Remember the scriptures I had you look up when Aunt Nelly died?"

"Yes."

"Well think about that. Now you'd better go back to bed." He pulled Brad tighter against him and then let him go. "Son, have you said your prayers?"

"No."

"Why don't you do that. We love you, son."

Brad nodded his head a little, turned and walked down the hall, his pajamas becoming darker. He turned off his light, but left his door half open.

Brad had been the only one of the kids old enough to visit Aunt Nelly in the hospital. A little more of her was gone each time, her body becoming more bone than flesh. Reed had always put his hand on Brad's shoulder as they walked silent to the car.

A man ought to be able to know that he would be resurrected the same way he knew that he was alive. It had to be the same kind of feeling. (I *know*, son, that through Jesus Christ all men are resurrected. We *live* after death. I *know* that. Accept my testimony. Don't ever worry about time or death; life is eternal.)

"Honey, was that Brad?" Marilyn stood in the kitchen doorway.

"Yes. He couldn't sleep. Clark drove by this afternoon and waved to him."

"Oh, he didn't tell me that." Marilyn walked over to Reed at the end of the sofa, hugged him, and then they both turned to look out through the screen. "I guess that he still remembers Aunt Nelly too."

"I guess he'd almost have to."

"Poor kid. It's been a sad day for a lot of people. When I think of Camille and those boys, I could cry. You never know how a day will end."

(His mother said often, "It isn't the dying that's hard, it's the living. We've all got to die sometime.

191

That's the Lord's plan.")

"I think I'll go out and water the lawn for a few minutes before I come to bed."

"Oh, honey, it's midnight."

"I'll only be a few minutes. I just want to catch two or three brown spots where the rainbird never gets."

"Well I'm going to bed; I'm tired. Don't be too long."

He kissed her. "Okay, I won't."

Reed stood on the front porch to roll up his pant legs. He turned on the water and pulled the hose out to the parking. Cold water dripped on his feet from the nozzle, and he spread his feet wider.

All the houses on the block were dark, and he named the sleeping families. The Staggs were the only family with a chain-link fence and outside lights at each corner of the house. Stagg had built a special underground fallout shelter with his house (a dentist, he had plenty of money). He had his own emergency power generator to go along with his year's supply. He had taught his whole family karate and how to shoot. Every three or four months Stagg stood up in testimony meeting and described what each family had to do to be safe now it was the last days and all the prophesies were being fulfilled, especially concerning the gathering of the Jews.

Reed moved from one brown spot to the next, the grass cool under his feet. His father, who did his whole lawn by hand, always watered his parking first so that by the time Reed's mother had finished the supper dishes, his father had moved back toward the porch. They sat on the steps together, held hands, the water from the nozzle dripping on the cement steps.

And when Reed and Marilyn went down in the

evenings to visit, old neighbors were out watering their lawns, but mostly women now. His mother told them who was sick, in the hospital, who had fallen and broken a hip, who was in intensive care, dying, or dead. He and Marilyn went to the viewings at the Berg and Walker Mortuaries, and sometimes they went to the funerals, joined the cortege to go to the cemetery. Every year he knew more people out in the cemetery. The cemetery had streets with addresses, and the corner markers were just like those in town. His parents went to more funerals now. They had more friends and relatives dead than alive.

Two weeks ago he had run his mother out to the cemetery to put flowers on Aunt Nelly's grave, and she met an old friend there she hadn't seen in over twenty years. They kissed each other, stood arm-in-arm looking east across the cemetery. "The morning of the resurrection will be wonderful," his mother said. Members of the Church were buried facing east.

Pulling the hose, Reed moved over to water the last brown spot, and he looked out between the houses to the valley lights and Utah Lake. A view lot was better than TV; the valley was always interesting, day or night, and you always had a sense of distance. He watched the valley lights, and then he pulled the hose back to the house and turned it off. Clark had a sprinkling system controlled by an electronic timer.

The rug was soft and warm under his naked feet again as he walked down the hall. Marilyn was asleep, the night lamp burning for him. He got clean pajamas and garments out of the dresser, went into their bathroom and closed the door.

Reed looked down at himself as he soaped under the warm spray. Through the washcloth he felt his bones under his flesh. He soaped twice, watched the last of the suds wash down the front of his legs and between his toes. He wiggled his toes. When he got out, he rubbed his body hard with his towel for the feeling (Clark had always used three and four towels when he showered after a game). Reed dropped the towel in the hamper and stood looking into the mirror. He moved his face closer, touched his teeth with his fingers, traced his jaw bone, felt his nose bone, the bone around his eyes, pressed against the thin flesh above his ear to feel his skull. He felt a faint pulse. Slowly he lowered his hand down to his heart to feel the steady beat. He stood for a moment longer, and then he put on his garments and pajamas.

He walked down the hall in the darkness to check the back and the carport doors, and then he locked the patio screen. The rising moon made the patches of trees and the cliffs on the mountains visible now. Morris Swensen, who was in the Geology Department, had told him that the earth's crust had broken for two hundred miles to form the Wasatch fault, one face rising ten thousand feet above the other. The mountains had resulted from thirty or maybe fifty million years of erosion by wind, water, and earthquakes. His neighbors on the east side of Pawnee Drive, the street highest on the mountain, sometimes found small boulders on their back lawns.

Reed turned and walked across the front room and down the hall. He pushed Brad's door open a little wider. Brad lay on his side, his sheet pushed down to the bottom of the bed. His radio was still on. Reed turned off the radio and then pulled the sheet up to cover Brad (both windows were open and the breeze had started). Brad opened his eyes, raised his head.

"It's okay, son," Reed said and put his hand on Brad's shoulder. "Everything's okay." Brad laid his head back down on the pillow and closed his eyes. Reed stood for a moment at the door then pulled it half shut. He checked the girls. They were asleep. He watched them for a moment, then turned down the hall.

When Reed got to his and Marilyn's bedroom, he switched off the night light, sat down on the bed, lifted his feet, and pulled the white clean sheet up to his chest. He lay there for a moment, everything in the house silent, staring up at the ceiling. He turned to Marilyn, who always slept on her side after the fourth or fifth month. He moved closer to her, her warmth, his body following hers, touching. Very carefully he put his hand on her side. The baby moved. Reed spread his fingers. The baby moved again, swam, strengthened himself. Reed closed his eyes and said his prayers.

ZARAHEMLA

"Dad, we're not going to stay overnight, are we, for sure?"

"Son, you father's told you that we'll be in Provo tonight. Now stop worrying about your baseball game tomorrow, please."

Jared glanced over at Sue, then turned back to the two-lane highway that cut along the base of the sagebrush-covered foothills edging the desert. They had left Las Vegas that morning, and Disneyland the day before. The side trip to Zarahemla would cost Brent one little league game if they stayed overnight. Craig, who sat by the other rear window, was in the city tennis tournament. Jared had promised they would not stay to visit. He looked at his watch.

Just before they left for California, Cory Jensen had called to say that he had another buyer for the stone house Jared's Great-grandfather Thatcher had built. A retiring Los Angeles doctor offered fifteen thousand cash for the house and the ten acres of land, and an extra thousand for the furniture. Every year the price climbed, yet Jared had never really put the house up for sale. Cory said the he would pay for the extra gas if Jared would stop in again.

Sue had said once more, "Make up your own mind, honey. It's your house."

They could put some of the money away for Craig's and Brent's missions and build a nice cabin on their lot in Provo Canyon with the rest. Many people in their ward had cabins, some as far away as Bear Lake. If a family didn't have a cabin, it had a camper, trailer, or motor-home, and some had boats. All of the houses in Indian Hills were new, and comfortable, and most of the families young. Their ward was one of the most active in the whole Church.

Jared had lived in the stone house with his mother and grandmother until he was eighteen. His great-grandfather had built a stone house for each wife—Nora, Etta, Emily, and Lily, Jared's great-grandmother. Jared's was the only house still in good repair and the only one still in the family. Each house had a row of six lombardy poplars and an iron fence across the front, a hedge of lilacs down one side, and was known by the wife's name.

He and Sue had planned to use the house summers, but his high-council position and her Sunday School teaching tied them down weekends. Craig and Brent didn't want to vacation in Zarahemla. His partner, Paul Terry, had bought his grandfather's farm in Nephi when he died, and Paul and his family spent a lot of time there. But Nephi was a lot closer than Zarahemla, and Paul's only boy, Jeff, was just eight. Paul's brother farmed it for him.

After Jared's grandmother died, Sue had wanted some of the furniture, but Jared didn't want to change anything that soon. To keep them from being stolen or lost, they took to Provo some porcelain pieces, the best handmade quilts, the family photo albums, and the large oval framed portrait photograph of his great-grandfather and his family (thirty-two children). Craig called it the polygamy picture and had it on the wall in his room. Craig wanted the brass bed too now.

Jared's grandmother had dusted the picture every day. She had been born in the house and lived in it all of her life. "My son," she said to him often, "your great-grandfather was one of the noblest men ever to draw a breath of air on this earth. He was God's servant, and if ever a man deserved the celestial kingdom, he did." Nathaniel Thatcher wore a full beard and his hair long, but he wasn't tall.

He had named Zarahemla, chosen the name of the greatest city in the Book of Mormon, been bishop for twenty-five years (was always called Bishop Thatcher), laid out the new town, built the new stone wardhouse, and sketched the scenes for its six stained-glass windows. He had built all of the original stone houses and town buildings in Zarahemla, dug the first canal, planted many of the trees, fed and fought the Indians, been judge and jury. He had run three farms, and he had healed the sick and called back the dying and the dead.

The last ten years of his life Nathaniel Thatcher had been a patriarch; Church members brought their children fifty and sixty miles by wagon to receive blessings under his hands. The last year, sitting up in the big brass bed, he had to reach out to lay his hands on the child's head. Brigham Young, God's prophet, stayed with him on his trips south through the villages in his white-topped wagon, the other wagons carrying the apostles, the special witnesses for Christ. "Be like your great-grandfather, my son," Jared's grandmother said, "for no boy ever had a nobler example. He held to the iron rod all of his life; he loved the Church."

In five generations his Great-grandfather Thatcher had ten thousand descendants, the blood brought over a millennium before to England by marauding Danes carried by him to the edge of an American desert. But the family was spread out now over the whole country, was not located in one village, that sense of blood, kinship, and order gone. The first two generations and most of the third were dead.

A white shaft of stone cut by Nathaniel Thatcher stood at the center of the family cemetery plot, which was enclosed by an iron fence. Every stone but three had embedded in it and sealed under glass the daguerreotyped face of the relative whose grave it was, proof that he or she would rise in that likeness on resurrection morning.

Behind Jared in the back seat, Brent was punching his baseball mitt again. Jared reached over to adjust the air conditioner (he wanted to turn it off; it kept him from smelling the sagebrush). He looked up at the paralleling mountains and then out to the desert, which showed patches of shadow now, the plateaus off toward the Colorado River beginning to turn blue. It was their first trip to Zarahemla this way. They always came down Pine Canyon from the north, which was the way his Great-grandfather Thatcher had led the thirty-two covered wagons from Provo, the iron-rimmed wheels scarring the canyon stone. Before Zarahemla, Nathaniel Thatcher had helped settle Provo and then had been called by President Brigham Young to leave his pregnant wife and five children to serve a mission in the South, make that sacrifice too.

He was hunted by mobs, tarred and feathered, shot at, arrested a dozen times, his journal full of accounts of the danger and persecution which made daily miracles necessary. But in those three years he converted over four hundred people to the gospel, each name carefully recorded in his journal: "This day I baptized and confirmed members of Christ's true church the following persons . . . . The mobs continue to hunt us from village to village." And now this convert posterity was part of the tremendous growth in the Church that latter-day prophets had foretold.

Sometimes in the evening, the light just right, Jared stood at his big picture window or on his back lawn to look southwest out across Provo, the valley, and Utah Lake to the silhouetted mountains and beyond. He had a wife, two sons, a partnership in an accounting business, a house, a position on the stake high council, and he had been on a mission.

Nathaniel Thatcher had preached for fifty years the latter-day restoration of the gospel, the prophetic calling of Joseph Smith, the truthfulness of the Book of Mormon. Balanced by his own common sense, he preached the fact of Christ's divine sonship, man's perfectibility, the resurrection, the gathering of the Jews, and the Saints' return to Zion in Jackson County, Missouri, to prepare for the millennium and Christ's reign on earth. He preached under the inspiration of the Holy Ghost, used his priesthood daily, and his faith became knowledge and then faith again as he faced some new impossibility requiring sacrifice, his journal full of the daily newness of it all.

His patriarchal blessing, given under the hands of the Prophet Joseph Smith's father, said that he would be a savior on Mount Zion among the Lamanite peoples. And he had preached the gospel to the Utes and Navahos, baptizing them in the desert water holes. Now the areas of greatest growth in the Church were Central and South America, where the Lamanite blood was most abundant. And the Church used language schools for the missionaries now, the standardized lesson approach, television, radio, films, exhibits at the world and national fairs, which were techniques that Jared hadn't even heard of when he was on his mission in Mexico. A man almost needed a Harvard M.B.A. to be a mission president now. Even after twenty years he still wished that he hadn't been called into the mission home to be secretary.

Jared glanced up into his rearview mirror. Craig and Brent lay back in their seats; they had stopped looking out their windows. The highway had begun to climb up through the foothills. Many of the Church leaders today had no pioneer past, so they didn't know the desert, mountains, and villages that way. Jared lowered his window and breathed in deep. He looked at his watch.

"I like the smell of the sagebrush," Sue said.

"It's always best after a rain." He closed the window. Provo had few really good smells.

Jared watched the shadows along the edge of the highway; the heat waves were gone now. He had been on the building committee for their new chapel. Based on the seven or eight basic plans permitted by the Church architect's office, all the new chapels were big, efficient, carpeted, air-conditioned—comfortable. They housed two and three wards, members going to meetings in shifts. Their Indian Hills chapel had high, narrow milkglass windows. He had wanted color. The evening sun coming through the windows of the old Zarahemla stone wardhouse filled the room with a hazy golden glow. And it was as if Brigham Young, the Prophet Joseph Smith, the Angel Moroni, the Father, the Son, and the other figures stood suspended in air, each window a vision.

A jack rabbit ran across the highway in front of the car. To the east the vast shadow-filled sandstone canyons dropped off toward the Colorado. The high west mountains were turning darker.

He had thought about selling the stone house when his grandmother died (he would rather sell than rent). His Aunt Laura, who had become the family genealogist after his grandmother, kept it as clean as she did her own. She did her genealogy there so she was in the house every day. His Uncle Charley farmed the ten acres along with his own place. He had tried at different times to raise fox, pheasants, mink, and turkeys, but he only made money on his crops and his few beef cattle. Jared had only cousins left in Zarahemla. Aunt Laura was his grandmother's niece, so was really only his cousin. His mother had been an only child. His Aunt Laura's two daughters lived in California.

"I hope that we don't have to stay more than an hour," Brent said. "Do we have to go to the cemetery again, Dad?"

"If we have time. It depends on how long the real estate man takes."

"Gee." Brent slumped back in his seat. Craig looked out at the desert again.

Jared watched the edge of the highway for ground squirrels and marmots. He had told Craig and Brent all of his grandmother's stories many times and tried to get them to remember the names of the most important faces in the old family photo albums. He had read to them from his typed copy of the journal, had told often the stories of his own boyhood, but they were older now. The main reason Paul had bought the old family farm was for his boy Jeff. Last week at the office he had talked again about moving to Nephi and commuting daily the eighty-mile round trip to Provo. "It would be worth it," he said.

Jared knew that Zarahemla had deteriorated since his own boyhood, as if the depression had continued. Many of the old houses were dilapidated, the lots trashy, the center of each block a jungle of hundred-and-twenty-year-old fruit trees, lilacs, hollyhocks, rotting pioneer barns and other outbuildings, and rusting junked cars and farm machinery. It was mostly the retired people moving in from Los Angeles and the other big urban areas that remodeled their houses for comfort and planted flower gardens.

Cory Jensen sold most of them their houses, and if not their houses then the solid pioneer furniture and brass beds they all wanted for their houses. He had a big circular "Antiques" sign outside of the store, and he searched the small towns for furniture. When Jared's mother worked at the store, old Bishop Jensen, Cory's father, sold only groceries and feed. He had been bishop of the Zarahemla Ward for twenty years, until the day he died.

"I just want to get home."

Sue turned. "We're all tired, Brent. We'll leave as soon as your father sees about selling the house." She turned back. "Look, there's Zarahemla now."

"Yes," Jared said.

The fields spread out from Zarahemla to meet the

desert. The river, a green line of cottonwoods, came out of the canyon, bent around Zarahemla and cemetery hill on the northeast and vanished down South Wash. Zarahemla was a dark green oval of trees; Nathaniel Thatcher wanted a city shaded from the sun by great trees. In Indian Hills a boy had no high trees. Jared turned his wrist to check the time, then looked above the highway to watch the Zarahemla trees grow more distinct.

It was always coolest under the cottonwoods along the river. He and his friends lay on their backs in the sand to watch the fluttering leaves. They carried water to the clay beds, wrestled and fought in the splendid wet cool red clay, became completely red, then ran and dived off the ledge. They cooked feasts of fresh corn, new potatoes, and trout, and they swam at night, lay in the sand under the incredibly starry desert sky, bodies alive even to the silence. The two times he had taken Craig and Brent down to the ledge hole to swim, they seemed almost afraid. They wore their trunks, didn't run and yell, didn't really enjoy the rope swing.

They didn't really enjoy staying in the stone house, except that Craig liked the brass bed. In Provo they had their friends, stereo, color TV, closets full of clothes, own rooms, and their league games. They both took swimming, diving, and tennis lessons again this summer. They studied hard in school (both he and Sue pushed that), and would go to college and into the professions.

They didn't need poverty or a depression to motivate them. The boys in Indian Hills expected to be presidents of corporations, doctors, lawyers, generals, cabinet members, or scientists, so counted on success always. The Church helped to breed that kind of ambition; doctrine, leadership, organization, programs, and dedication had become the most important things now.

When Craig and Brent were younger, on the return trip from Zarahemla Jared always tried to drive through Manti after dark. He wanted them to see the lighted temple their great-grandfather had sacrificed two years of his life to help build. On the hill, brilliant white in the darkness, it seemed like part of a celestial city. Sue always told the story again of how Moroni in the Book of Mormon had dedicated the hill fifteen hundred years earlier as a temple site. The same Moroni, now a resurrected angel, appeared to the boy Joseph Smith and led him to the golden plates.

The highway cut down out of the sagebrush foothills and into the flat green fields. Jared slowed down to fifty.

The new Provo and Ogden temples looked almost alike. Every day driving to work Jared had seen the big white sign listing the architects and contractors for the Provo temple. He knew that the Church's real strength was in the urban areas like Salt Lake, Los Angeles, Boston, and Washington D.C., and that it had been for fifty years. Membership had increased five or six times since his own birth.

The Church had developed in the last twenty years the new administrative know-how and standardized programs to run the big urban wards. The big new twenty-eight story central office building housed nearly three thousand salaried clerks, secretaries, and administrators. The journal said: "God will prosper his saints in this land, and all the valleys will be filled with a righteous people."

"There's Uncle Charley's, boys," Sue said. "See the trees?"

A mile northeast across the fenced fields, the high clump of trees stood black-green, and beyond that a half a mile the line of six poplars marked the stone house. Jared's Uncle Charley's place (his Aunt Laura had inherited some land) was part of Nathaniel Thatcher's east farm. Jared had told Craig and Brent how he had plowed, harrowed, planted, irrigated, hoed, fixed fence, and how he had put up hay for fifteen and sixteen hours straight. His body tired to numbness, he saw across the fields in the moonlight the order he had helped create.

Jared's grandmother had taught him to save nearly every dime he earned. Every fall she took him to Salt Lake to buy his school clothes with some of his saved money. They visited relatives to search for genealogy, toured President Brigham Young's houses, climbed the hill to his grave, toured Temple Square, and sat in the tabernacle to hear the great organ. And his grandmother stopped him three or four times in the city to look up at the golden Moroni standing on the temple's highest spire and holding the golden trumpet to his lips (no angel stood on the top of the Provo temple spire, which he saw from his valley-view window).

Each trip she narrated for him again how President Brigham Young had called his great-grandfather to leave Provo six months after his return from his mission and build a new city on the edge of a desert. Pointing out through the bus window, both coming and going, she described the journey for him, and she told him what each state historical marker said as they passed it. "The Prophet needed a man with a lot of good common sense and great faith," she said.

The youngest daughter of the fourth and youngest wife, she was not born until twenty years after it all happened. Yet she spoke of it as if the cooking-fire ashes were still warm, the wagon tracks visible in the sand, the trail graves new, and the songs and prayers of thanksgiving audible on the night breeze: "Today, the Sabbath, the company rested. We spent our time in singing praises to God, and bearing testimony to his work in the latter-day kingdom. Thus we renewed our minds and bodies to his service." Jared had searched in Pine Canyon to find the wagon-wheel marks cut in the stone.

"They were faithful, my son; always remember that," she told him. It pleased her when he named all of the faces in the polygamy picture and in the albums. Sitting between her and his mother in sacrament meeting as a boy, he looked up at the glowing windows and expected always to find his great-grandfather among the figures. (The six spaces had been filled with clear glass for the twenty years it took the Zarahemla saints to raise the money to have the windows made in Italy.) The whole emphasis now for a boy in the Church was youth leadership, chastity, testimony, and mission preparation.

At the canal bridge Jared turned right and off the highway. The shadows from the willows along the bank edged the road. In the fall after the water was shut off, he had pitchforked the trout in the shallow pools and carried them home in a gunnysack. They passed Carter's place and then the Johnson's. Five families lived on the canal road east of the highway. One evening when Craig said it was impossible to know everybody in a town, Jared drew a street map of Zarahemla and named every family. He could have named the children and told which families were related. He saw their faces still.

"It's sure a dusty road," Brent said. "Why don't they have good roads like in Provo, and lawns?

"Stop complaining," Craig said.

"I ain't complaining."

The barn and other outbuildings stood fifty yards behind the red-brick house. Jared lifted his foot off the gas pedal and turned in the driveway. He and Sue rolled down their windows. As he braked the car to a stop, his Aunt Laura, just as he knew she would be, was out the back door of the house before he had turned off the key. The heat entered the car.

"Well, here we are, Aunt Laura," Sue said out her window. When they got out, his Aunt Laura kissed and hugged them all and told them that Uncle Charley was still out cutting hay. "He'll be in for supper, she said. "We thought we'd have an early supper out on the back lawn in the shade."

Jared looked at his watch. "I want to stop by the house for a minute before I see Cory Jensen, so I'd better go."

"Oh, Jared, are you going to sell? Do you think he will, Sue?"

"Well, we're still thinking about building a cabin, but Jared's never really offered the place for sale. He has to decide, Aunt Laura."

"I know, I know. His grandmother will turn over in her grave. If only we had somebody in the family who needed a place to rent."

"I'll be back as soon as I can."

"Don't let me forget, Jared. I've got copies of some new family group sheets for you before you go back. We ought to have the boys come down and do baptisms for the dead this fall."

"That would be nice, Aunt Laura. Craig has been to the new Provo temple once to do baptisms." Sue turned toward the house.

"I've got ice-cold Kool-Aid in the house. Why don't you folks stay overnight? We'd love to have you."

Jared switched off the air conditioner when he got out on the road so that he could smell the cut hay. He drove slowly, looked out across the fields for his Uncle Charley on the tractor. His Uncle Charley had spent his whole life in Zarahemla, and many times out in fields working he had told Jared not to return after he finished college. "Even if you could make a decent living," he said, "your kids would be gone the minute they were old enough, just like mine. You've had the best of it while you're young." Jared knew twenty or thirty men in their Indian Hills ward who had grown up on small farms in Utah and southern Idaho.

Down the road the six poplars outside the iron fence threw their long shadows across to the canal. Grey gravel dust covered the weeds and willows.

He had wanted to go to college at B.Y.U., but he went to the University of Utah because that's where his state scholarship was. It was his first time away from Zarahemla, and he could not comprehend the students who spent their days and nights trying to cleanse themselves of everything Mormon. In their dedicated rage to change their way of feeling and knowing, they turned to gambling, drunkenness, fornication, homosexuality, or they dedicated their lives to science, literature, psychology, and art. They forbade themselves any longer to be limited by the injunction to be perfect, denied prophets and revelation. They cursed the idea that man could progress through the eternities to become like God, and so denied what for him had already become blood.

Jared braked as he drove into the shade from the poplars, turned in the driveway, and drove up to the hollyhocks and stopped. He got out and stood looking at the lawn and the house. The hollyhocks were in bloom. He walked across the lawn (he had always cut the lawn on Saturday for Sunday), went up on the porch, pulled back the screen and unlocked the door with the key he kept on his ring.

His Aunt Laura's genealogy sheets lay on the round table. He smelled the coolness. He listened. His mother had been dead fifteen years, and his grandmother half that time. He touched the sofa. He touched the clean curtains. He touched the stone above the fireplace. In the kitchen he touched the table, stove, and walls. He opened the drawers and cupboards. He turned on the cold-water faucet to hear the sound. He went down into the cellar just for the smell that never changed winter or summer, and to see the shelves of empty fruit jars. Each summer Sue wanted some of the jars. His grandmother made it almost a sacrament when they ate fruit from the old glass-topped jars that had been her mother's.

She said: "We all have great reason to be grateful. We have food to eat, clothes to wear, a good roof over our heads; we have the iron rod of the gospel to cling to, and we have the family."

Jared went back upstairs. In the hall he pushed open the doors to his grandmother's bedroom (the old star quilt was on her bed), then his mother's, stood for a moment in each doorway, and pushed open the door

211

to his own room last. The brass bed shone in the sunlight coming through the windows below the half-pulled blinds. On spring nights the scent of lilacs filled his room, and always, except in winter, there was the smell of lawn, trees, and fields. He heard the night birds, the crickets, and the wind and storm in the poplars. He saw in the darkness blurred shapes of furniture. If he put out his hands he touched quilts his grandmother or great-grandmother, or both of them, had made, and he touched the bed's cool metal.

Jared looked at his watch. He closed his bedroom door. He turned and walked down the hall and through the front room, but stopped by the round table. He bent and leafed through the family group sheets to read the new names and their dates. He looked up at the large white oval spot above the fireplace where the polygamy picture had hung.

Even during his boyhood the family had already been gone into the cities for twenty-five years, the farms divided too often to be productive, the sense of blood dissipated. But his grandmother named and described the houses and fields as if they still belonged to the family. After the stories and the pictures, she brought out the collected patriarchal blessings for him to read. He scraped and painted the iron fence around the family graves, cut the grass, and raked the fall leaves, the faces in the embedded pictures watching him. While his grandmother washed the headstones, she described how the family would visit among the open graves on the morning of the first resurrection.

For fifteen years his grandmother made temple burial clothes to earn money for his mission and college savings account, which she had started by mail the day of his birth. (His father, who was from Price, had been killed there in a coal mine three months before he was born.) She filled the house with the smells of cooking, baking, bottling, and ironing, smells he would remember all of his life, smell for a boy as important as sight or sound. When he returned from school in the silent afternoons to change his clothes and go to work over at his uncle's, he often found a note on the kitchen table: "My son, I have gone to help Sister Johnson." Or it would be some other neighbor or relative. Wherever there was need in Zarahemla, his grandmother helped, charity a required part of existence because they had no doctor, hospital, or mortuary. And when she returned she told him stories of birth, suffering, death, of the holy Melchizedek priesthood's power to heal and to restore life. She told him too of the dead returning from paradise in dreams and visions to comfort the living.

Jared straightened the family group sheets on the table. Their ward youth council had a committee to plan monthly service projects. Craig was chairman. In Indian Hills families had life, health-and-accident, maternity, and disability insurance, and retirement programs. Paul had said to him last Christmas, "You have to be careful, Jared, or a kid grows up feeling the whole world's rich. They don't know where money comes from any more. I know boys eighteen years old who have lived in comfort all their lives and have yet to do a real day's work. Yet the Church sends them on missions."

He and Paul had been in the Mexican Mission together. He hoped that Craig and Brent would be able to stay out in the field and not end up in the mission home. He and Sue had decided that if he sold the house, what money the boys didn't have saved would come from that. If they would save for their missions, he would pay for their college.

Jared stood by the front room table listening, head raised, then turned and walked out the open front door, closed and locked it, holding the screen back with his shoulder.

Jared drove slowly because of the dust, had the visor down against the direct hot sunlight. He didn't honk at the people he knew because they wouldn't recognize the car, and he didn't have time to stop. He didn't know any of the kids. He slowed down when he passed Aunt Etta's place, which somebody had boarded up, the poplars still alive because they were on the ditch. The lawn was dry weeds. Jared turned the corner. Trees protected each of the two or three houses on each block. Except for the occasional garden, all the vacant lots were dry weeds.

He was thirty before he had understood that southeastern Utah could not have been beautiful to the pioneers who came from England, northern Europe, and the American East. They could have had no affinity for heat, sandstone, alkali, sagebrush, and sandy irrigated farms. Diphtheria took whole families of children together, or killed one child every year. Israelites in the wilderness, the pioneers had their Canaan and their Zion in green Missouri, where it rained. Two and three generations had to die out before the fear of the arid land passed.

Nathaniel Thatcher wrote in his journal the name of the man who killed a neighbor in his own garden with a shovel because of a stream of irrigation water. He preached for fifty years against theft and the other sins—drunkenness, lust, ignorance, hate, pride, and sloth, and all of his life he sought forgiveness of his own sins. Men were excommunicated, flogged (a group of older Zarahemla boys out cutting wood murdered two friendly Indians and hid their bodies), but only a man's spilt blood washed away some of his sins forever. On one of the trips to Salt Lake, he and his grandmother stopped in Provo, and she took him to the B.Y.U. library to see the seven volumes of his great-grandfather's journal. "Pick them up, son," she said. "Hold them, open them. See how beautifully he wrote. Even his handwriting was beautiful."

Jared turned the corner at Larsen's station and drove down Main Street, which was asphalted now. He drove past the chapel. (He didn't take Craig and Brent in the early evenings now to see the Father, Son, Holy Ghost, and the prophets made alive by the sun's last rays.) Zarahemla had one block of stores, Christensen's and Jensen's the only two not boarded up. Everybody drove up the canyon and over to Richfield to shop. A "Real Estate" sign hung from the big "Antiques" sign. Heat filled the car again when he parked. He got out and walked past the old plows, milk cans, stoves, and wagon wheels lining the front of the store. He'd always ridden his bike when he came to see his mother. He pushed open the door.

"Well, hello, Jared. How are you? Back again I see." Mrs. Williams stood behind the candy case helping two boys.

"Yes," he said.

"Mr. Jensen's back in the office waiting for you."

"Thanks, I'll go back." He walked past the old furniture; the store smell was different.

Cory saw him through the window and came to

215

the door to shake his hand and lead him into the office. "Sit down, Jared, sit down. It's good to see you." They talked about his mother and grandmother, and Cory asked how his Aunt Laura and Uncle Charley were.

"Look, Jared, I appreciate your coming by, especially since you don't have that place up for sale yet, which I understand perfectly."

"I suppose that you sell most of what's sold."

"Well, most of it I guess. People see your house, look through the windows, and come to me." Cory opened his desk drawer. "I've got two cashier's checks here and they're made out to you. One is for the house and land, and the other for the furniture, if you'll sell that too." He laid the checks on the desk by Jared's hand.

Jared read his name on both checks. "The doctor seems willing to pay for what he wants, doesn't he."

"Look, Jared, you're a CPA, so you know this is a good deal. I don't think you'll ever get a better one."

"I guess I probably never will."

"To tell you the truth, Jared, I don't know from one day to the next how much longer people will want these old places. It's too lonely down here. Half of them are up for sale again in a year or two. The doctor said that any changes to the house will all be in the original stone, which ought to make you happy. He wants to retire here and raise Arabians. He's a member of the Church from Los Angeles."

Jared touched both checks. "He sounds like a man who would take care of the place, I guess."

Cory opened his desk drawer again. "I've got a quit-claim deed made out to you. You can take these checks right along with you." Jared took the deed and read the two names. "Sixteen thousand is a lot of money, Jared, even today. You could take your wife and boys to Hawaii for a nice vacation, buy a new car, a couple of new color TV's, and still have money left over. You could be real comfortable."

Jared looked up at Cory, and then he laid the deed back down on the desk.

"You know, Jared, Charley and Laura won't be able to take care of your place forever, and you don't get down to use it."

"No they won't."

"Look, I don't want you to think I'm pushing you, but his doctor has an option on another place over in Sanpete Valley. He likes your place the best though, and he'll pay my commission."

"How long is he willing to wait?"

"He said a week."

"Selling now makes a lot of sense to me, Jared."

"I guess it does." He stood up. "Well, it's something to keep thinking about."

Cory picked up the checks. "I'd sure like to see you take these with you, Jared, but I don't want to push. You know what you want to do."

Cory walked him to his car, his hand on his shoulder. As Jared backed out, Cory waved. He'd offered to pay for the extra gas.

Jared drove back the way he had come. On the canal road, he slowed down when he came to the poplars, looked at his watch, and turned in the driveway again. He got out of the car and walked past the lilacs and around to the back, and sat on the porch. The blue plateaus, line of river trees, fields, and cemetery hill had not yet begun to vanish, but the air was cooler. In the last horizontal shafts of evening sunlight, the headstones sometimes shown like win-

217

dows into the earth. His grandmother always told him the life stories of the old people whose funerals she took him to. Jared watched a magpie light on the back fence, teeter for a moment, and then fly away. Suffering and death nearly always came by surprise in Indian Hills. Neither Craig nor Brent had ever been to a funeral.

(It would not have surprised him then, a boy, to have had one of his dead relatives knock on the door and ask for his grandmother, or for him. His grandmother took him often to Manti to be baptized for the dead.)

The gospel didn't require a man and woman to sacrifice their lives overcoming the arid land now. The whole emphasis was on the new Church programs in education, social services, chapel construction, missionary work, welfare, genealogy, and family life, which met the new needs. Now the general authorities were nearly all former lawyers, businessmen, or educational administrators, most of them born in the twentieth century.

The new excitement for Craig and Brent would be in the leadership necessary for a world Church. Their missions would not be like his had been. He had not used a standard lesson program, flip-cards, film strips, tapes, and referral system. Now the Church had fifteen thousand missionaries out and was building a big new language training mission at B.Y.U. Thirty, forty, fifty thousand missionaries, whatever it took, would carry the universal gospel to every corner of the earth. Their ward had fifteen missionaries out (he had been the only missionary from the Zarahemla Ward in two years); four members of their ward were mission presidents.

Paul said: "How do you know what a kid feels about the Church if you don't know it's what you felt? How do you talk to a kid about anything today? They don't grow up the same here in Provo."

Sitting there on the porch, Jared reached out to touch the railing. He stood up and touched the stone wall; he traced the still-visible chisel marks with his finger tips: "Today we began to build Lily's house. We will finish it by September so that she can be comfortable and have her own place like my other three wives." Nathaniel Thatcher blessed and dedicated each stone house.

He gave patriarchal blessings in the front room (he had known the Prophet Joseph Smith, been driven out of Nauvoo by mobs. He had crossed the plains with those first companies in 1847, been called on a mission by Brigham Young, and then sent to build a city). He told each child his Biblical blood inheritance (Dan, Benjamin, Joseph, Judah), what God proposed for him if he proved faithful and ordered his life. In those last ten years he gave over five hundred blessings, his mind clear until the day he died. Jared spread both his hands flat to touch the stone, touched his forehead against it.

Nathaniel Thatcher was ninety-two, his three oldest wives and nearly half his children dead before him, and he died in the brass bed in a stone house he had built nearly fifty years before. And after a hundred years that house was still silent in a storm. In Indian Hills men, after work, planted lawns and frail new trees, erected grape-stake fences, put in patios, and finished their basements to make their homes more comfortable.

Jared turned on the porch and looked toward Pine

Canyon. Looking out his valley-view window, he sometimes blotted out all Provo below him. He made it all again sagebrush, grass, and willows. Near the river stood Fort Utah and the log cabins. The thirty-two covered wagons stood lined up, tops white in the morning sunlight. A small herd of cattle grazed off to the side. Nathaniel Thatcher knelt with the company, leading them in prayer: "Today we began our journey, which we asked God to bless. We pray for the faith and good sense necessary to our tasks. With God's help, it will be so."

Stonemason, farmer, bishop, architect, explorer, Indian agent, father, husband to four wives, man of God under a prophet's mandate, he led them all to face the daily reality of life in the arid land. They would sacrifice to help build the kingdom of God on this earth, their faith as useful and necessary to them as the water they would bring down from the river onto their crops, their visions and daily lives grand. (Using rocks and small logs, Jared had covered the clearest set of wagon tracks cut in the canyon rock to keep them from weathering.)

He looked at his watch, walked off the porch and around the house to the car. He backed out to the iron fence then stopped to let a pickup tear by. The long cloud of grey warm dust blurred the road and reached the front edge of the lawn. Jared waited; he didn't roll up the windows. Zarahemla and many of the other rural pioneer Utah towns had been dead now for over forty years, since the big exodus. The rural town and county governments were poor, inefficient, the services all substandard or nonexistent. Most of the wards had gone to seed, the possessions of a few active families. The small towns had the highest per capita liquor consumption in the state, the most people on welfare, and had high rates of juvenile delinquency, divorce, premarital pregnancy, and suicide. Boredom and poverty drove out the young. Some land was being bought up by outside money for recreational development now, and in some areas there was interest in the coal deposits. Jared let up on the brake and eased the car out onto the road.

When he got back, Craig and Brent were in the house watching a baseball game on TV; they'd eaten early except for dessert. The spread table was under the big boxelder tree; where Aunt Laura always had it. "It's good to see you, son," his Uncle Charley said as they shook hands. "How are you getting along?" His uncle held his hand in both of his.

"Good, Uncle Charley, thank you." He sat down next to Sue at the table. It was cool again under the big boxelder.

"Well, it's all been blessed, so let's eat. Jared, you must be starved." His Aunt Laura handed him the potato salad, then the fresh corn, hot biscuits, and the sliced ham. Sue poured his Kool-Aid. He told them what Cory Jensen had said about the option and what the doctor wanted to do with the place.

"He'll pay Cory's commission too. I guess he really wants it."

"Son, we're glad to look after the place for you like we have, but we can't guarantee anything any more. People come in and steal these old places empty. They even take the doors."

"It's awful," his Aunt Laura said.

"That's a good price for around here. Cory's still honest."

"Oh, Charley, don't encourage him. I just can't

221

think of anybody but family living in that house. Jared, you didn't get any tomatoes." She handed him the plate of sliced fresh tomatoes. "If only we had somebody in the family who needed to rent a place."

"A cabin in Provo Canyon makes a lot more sense for Jared and Sue. A thing has to be used."

"These darn flies." His aunt waved her hand over the ham. "Remember how upset your grandmother used to get with these flies, Jared? Oh, how she hated flies."

"What do you think about selling this time, Sue?"

"It's still Jared's decision, Uncle Charley. He knows how he feels."

"Well, it's the only sensible thing to do now I think. Jared, you ought to bring your boys down and work in the hay with me for two or three weeks. That would toughen you up a little."

"I'd like that, Uncle Charley, but I don't know about the boys."

"Oh, they'd get used to it after a few days. Craig worked hard freezing the ice cream."

Jared turned in his chair. Covered with wet gunnysacks, the old hand-cranked wooden freezer stood at the corner of the house on the cement. It had always been his job to freeze the ice cream. Water darkened the cement around the freezer. He turned back. His aunt was talking to Sue.

He had stopped telling Craig and Brent his stories about work. Sports taught them their bodies and how expert they were, for there was no real physical work for them to do in Indian Hills.

In the late afternoon, his body wet from swimming in the river, he had run with the other boys across new-plowed fields to fight their spring wars, the soft clods exploding against their bodies. Exhausted finally, they would lie down in the sun-warmed loam, vanish in the brownness, looking up at the blue sky, watching the white circling gulls.

His sons' work was to learn to play the piano, earn college scholarships, and be active in the Church and develop strong testimonies. They needed to prepare themselves for their missions, and after that for marriage, college, and post-graduate work. Their generation would be the new bishops, stake presidents, mission presidents, and other leaders the expanding world Church needed. And they would be successful doctors, lawyers, scientists, professors, and businessmen.

"It's too bad you can't get one of those house-movers to take your house to Provo, Jared."

His Uncle Charley laughed.

"Oh, Charley, Jared knows what I mean. Don't you Jared?"

He looked at his Uncle Charley. "Yes, Aunt Laura."

"Well, Craig certainly wants the brass bed for his room." Sue put a spoonful of jello salad on her plate.

"It was the bed Jared's Great-grandfather Thatcher died in, Sue."

"Yes, I know."

"An apostle spoke. It was a wonderful funeral. People came from all over the county."

They listened to his aunt tell the story. Sue poured Jared more Kool-Aid.

("My wife Lily nurses and cares for me. God will take me home. I have done his work.") In the brass bed twelve children had been conceived and born. Four had died in infancy, but the earth still replenished. At the side of the bed, kneeling, Nathaniel Thatcher had said his thousands of prayers. Nathaniel Thatcher spent one month with each of his four wives and her family. And each wife sent him to the next wife with his basket of clean clothes, and with fresh loaves of bread and fresh pies in the wagon. Every day of his life in Zarahemla, Jared had seen one or more of the three other stone houses. He walked through the two already abandoned, stood in the dusty rooms, listened, saw the broken furniture, reached out to touch the other brass beds.

"It was wonderful, Jared," his aunt said, "just wonderful."

"Yet, it was." He drank his Kool-Aid.

"Oh, son," she said, "I forgot to tell you. They tore down Aunt Nora's house."

Jared lowered his glass.

His uncle took the last slice of tomato. "Some Salt Lake lawyer wanted the cut stone for a house. The walls was all that was standing anyway. He took the iron fence too."

"It's awful," his aunt said, "just awful."

"They even buy old barns and sheds for wood to line rooms with. Hell."

Jared set his glass on the table.

Craig came around the corner of the house. "It's a slow game," he said sitting down at the table. "Six errors already."

"Where's Brent, son?"

"Oh, he's still watching."

Jared looked at his watch. "Go get him, son, will you. Your Aunt Laura's ready to serve the ice cream and cake, and then we've got to go." He put his hand on Craig's shoulder. "We don't want to get to Provo at midnight, do we?"

"That's a fine looking boy you've got there, Jared."

"Yes he is, Uncle Charley."

Just before they finished their dessert, his Aunt Laura brought from the house the copies of the new family group sheets for them. "When the boys come down to do the baptisms, Sue, you and Jared can do the endowments."

"It would be nice to be in the Manti temple as a family, Aunt Laura."

They were in the car and ready to go just before seven. His Uncle Charley and Aunt Laura stood at Sue's window. "Remember now, Jared, your Uncle Charley and I are as happy as we can be to look after the house. Don't worry about that a minute."

"I know, Aunt Laura. Thank you."

"You're going to go by the cemetery."

"No, I don't think we'll take time now."

Sue turned to look at him.

"Well, maybe next time then. We love you all. You know that. Come again soon."

"We will, Aunt Laura."

Standing on the lawn, his uncle and aunt waved until Jared had backed out and turned up the road toward the highway. He and Sue closed their windows against the dust, and he turned on the air conditioner.

At the canal bridge they got back on the asphalt. Brent wanted to stop at Jensen's Store to get some candy, but Sue said he had just had ice cream and cake. The "Antiques" sign was made from the top of a round table.

They left the houses and the trees, drove out through the west fields, the highway paralleling the river for a mile. Jared lowered his window to smell the cottonwoods that rose up through the foothills. They passed the "Historical Marker Ahead" sign, and then the "View Area" sign. The highway widened to the right, the white line curving that way. Jared slowed a little, looked back over his shoulder toward Zarahemla, then pushed up the directional signal.

"Oh, Dad, do we have to stop again?"

"It's a good view, son, this time of evening. It's the last time to see Zarahemla."

Sue turned. "We'll only be a minute, Brent."

"Ah gee."

Jared parked, and they all got out. He and Sue read again the brass plaque set in the stone column, and then they walked over and stood at the edge of the hill. The dark fields spread out from the darker oval of Zarahemla trees and cemetery hill to the desert, the river a thin dark line of trees. The great sandstone plateaus, blue and pink now, lifted above the shadowed canyons to the horizon.

Thirty-two wagons had pulled down out of the canyon and stopped here: "Praise God, we have come to the end of our journey. Here we will build a city at the edge of the desert. We will call the city Zarahemla." And all that afternoon the white gulls, come up from the river, followed the plows in white flocks. By the next day Nathaniel Thatcher had surveyed a ditch, and brought water from the river to soften some of the ground to make the plowing easier.

It became a town, not a city. But it was beautiful then—the houses built, trees, grass, and gardens planted, the yards all fenced, order visible. The irrigated fruitful fields, the herds of sheep and cattle in the mountains, the growing families all proved faith and works triumphant against the arid land, God's mercy and bounty known to his chosen people. (Last week after they hired the new full-time accountant, Paul said, "I'm investing every dime. Judy and I want to retire early and move back to Nephi and the farm. It may be too late for Jeff, but the grandkids will have a place to come to. It's the only way to live." Every weekend Paul went down to work on remodeling the house to make it more comfortable. He and his family often went to church in Nephi.)

Sue put her arm through Jared's. "It must have all seemed very new and wonderful once."

"Yes, I'm sure it did."

Brent was throwing rocks to see how far he could get them out over the hill. Craig, arms folded, stood looking toward the desert.

"I'll call Cory Jensen tomorrow and tell him we've decided to sell." He turned to look at Sue. "You surprised?"

"No, not really." She squeezed his arm a little.

"I didn't think you would be. It makes the most sense, I guess."

"You don't want to spend the money on the cabin either, do you?"

"No."

"You want to keep the money for the boys' missions."

"That won't take all of it."

"Maybe they'll call you to be a mission president."

"I don't want to be a mission president, but I'd like to go on another mission with you after Brent's in college. I'd like to work in a small Mexican town or a village. You'd have to learn Spanish. The Church is going to be sending a lot more older couples."

"It sounds exciting."

Jared put his arm around Sue's shoulder, and they stood watching the colors and shadows change. "We'll keep the furniture and other things you want. We can refinish some pieces for Craig and Brent and store them till they get married. It's all good stuff."

He saw his watch. He took his arm from around Sue's shoulder and held her hand. "Come on boys, let's go." Brent ran back to the car ahead of them and slammed his door shut.

A mile above the historical marker, they passed the place where Jared had covered the wagon tracks cut in the rock. The air conditioner off, through the open windows came the cool smell of the pines, quaking aspen, and the river.

Douglas Thayer grew up in Provo, Utah. In 1946 he quit high school to join the U. S. Army, serving in Germany during the occupation. Eighteen months after his discharge, he returned to Germany as a Mormon missionary. He graduated from Brigham Young University in 1955 with a major in English. He later took a Master of Arts degree in American Literature at Stanford University and a Master of Fine Arts degree in creative writing at the University of Iowa.

He has been a clerk-typist, a janitor, a steel worker, a seasonal ranger in Yellowstone National Park, an insurance salesman, a construction laborer, and a driller's helper. Since 1957 he has taught in the English Department at Brigham Young University, where he currently directs the creative writing program. He has won several prizes for his published fiction, and in 1972 he received the Karl G. Maeser Creative Arts Award.

Thayer's short stories have appeared singly in the *Improvement Era*, the *Ensign, Sunstone, Colorado Quarterly, Prairie Schooner, Brigham Young University Studies,* and *Dialogue.* His story "The Turtle's Smile" was listed in *The Best American Short Stories* 1971. *Under the Cottonwoods and Other Mormon Stories* is the first published collection of his work. He is now finishing a Mormon novella and a collection of short stories set in the Rocky Mountain West.

Active in the Mormon Church all of his life, Thayer serves as a counselor in a Provo ward bishopric. He is married to the former Donlu DeWitt, and they have two children, Emmelyn and Paul.